VALLEY OF THE KINGS

Written by

Bernice H.Z.M.

BERNICE H.Z.M.

Pharaoh Khai was a great King who ascended the throne at the age of nine. He quickly gained the respects of the royal court members and his people by the age of eighteen. On his twentieth birthday, he invited royalties and noblemen across lands and oceans. There, he met Prince Sevrin of Warania.

Modern day Archaeologist Dr Shohan, led a team of experts on an expedition to uncover the tomb of the last King of Egypt, Pharaoh Kai Tutankhamen.

CHAPTER 1

1500 B.C.

Khai stood in front of a full-length mirror, watching as chambermaids attended to his daily attire. He had a white kilt wrapped around his waist, secured with a sash, a side slit revealing his muscular thigh.

He lowered his head slightly for a chambermaid to put a headdress on him, its blue and white striped silk cloth draped down to his shoulders while a small golden snakehead ornament decorated the centre of his headdress.

He had eyes lined with black kohl, biceps clad with jewelleries of gold bangles that complemented his bronze skin. He also wore a gold bedazzling necklace with the brightest ruby that hung right at his sternum.

"Pharaoh Khai, my King."

The chambermaids left, and Khai turned to face his royal advisor.

"The King of Warania and his Prince have come bearing gifts," said the royal advisor.

As Khai walked out of his chamber, two Egyptian guards with spears as tall as them bowed their heads.

Khai halted and turned back to his two guards. "Do not let anyone into my chamber. Not even Princess Nari."

The two guards bowed their heads once more and said in unison, "Yes, my King."

His royal advisor frowned at him as they made their way to the throne room. "My King, forgive me for being intrusive. But the Great Pharaoh of Egypt needs an heir." He walked as fast as his short and stubby legs could carry, keeping up with his King. "The Queen Mother will be displeased if she hears that Princess Nari has never once been in your chambers—"

Khai turned around and his royal advisor almost slammed against him. "My mother only arranged my marriage with the Princess to tighten our allies with the East. I have no intention to have her bear my child," Khai spat and the royal advisor quickly lowered his head. Khai smirked when he saw him tremble slightly. "I'm sure Princess Nari has no objections."

The royal advisor knew better than to speak more.

Seated on his gold pleated throne embedded with rubies and thousands of diamonds, Khai waved over for a servant. The servant approached with a golden tray with a chalice of wine.

"Her majesty has arrived," the royal advisor announced.

Khai rolled his eyes as his mother entered to take her seat beside Khai, her throne just as bedazzling as his. "Mother," he greeted grumpily.

"It's your birthday today. Who knows a King may come bearing their daughters for a hand in marriage," the Queen Mother chided.

"I have no interest in any more marriages," Khai clicked his tongue and placed his wine cup down. "I'm only interested in rare treasures. Treasures where there is only one in the world. Not princesses who do nothing but only bear a pawn for your muse, Mother." Khai smiled smugly when the Queen Mother frowned in his direction.

"The King of Warania and his Prince." The royal advisor announced.

A burly King sauntered into the hall with the prince following right by his side. Servants rolled in barrels and wagons of chests, laying them down before the King and before taking their leave.

"Ah, King Sejong," The Queen Mother greeted, leaving her throne and giving the King a warm welcome hug. "And I see your Prince has grown up into a handsome fine young man," she walked over and gave the prince a peck on his cheek. "You were just a tiny little infant when I visited your mother and father twenty years ago."

That caught Khai's attention. The King and his Prince wore a different kind of attire. While the male royalties in Egypt wore silken kilt around their waists, the prince standing before him wore a robe that covered the entire length of his body. He had a piece of silken band wrapped around his slim waist. He also had the fairest skin Khai had ever seen.

"Greetings, your Majesty," The Prince bowed down and through the small opening of the prince's collar, Khai thought he saw what seemed like gold body chains starting from his necklace. "I am Prince Sevrin from Warania. I have come bearing gifts for your birthday. I have heard that Pharaoh Khai, the great King of Egypt, indulges in rare treasures."

Khai watched as the prince knelt to unveil a chest full of gold statues.

Khai smirked at the prince. "And by any chance, are you part of the gifts?"

Present day

"Dr. Shohan!" Bentley shouted and waved him over.

Shohan had been taking a short rest under the man-made tent while dusting off newly uncovered artifacts.

"Dr. Shohan! You have to see this!" Bentley shouted again and Shohan stood up, dusting the desert sand off his attire.

"What have we found this time?" Shohan spoke into the dug-up tunnel. He found Bentley squatting inside the tunnel with his helmet lights on.

"You will never believe this. I think we found another tomb!" Bentley's eyes glimmered, chest heaving with a shovel in one hand.

Shohan nodded and gestured for Bentley to come back up. "Okay. Come on up for a rest now, I'll take over. Inform Dr. Layton about this," Shohan took the helmet lights and shovel from Bentley and began climbing down the ladder into the tunnel.

Shohan started prodding the tip of the shovel around the tomb entrance, more rubble fell and clouds of dust swirled around the limited confines. Shohan wrapped a towel around his lower face and began tearing down the entrance.

"Bentley said we found a new tomb entrance?"

Shohan turned to see Dr. Layton just climbing down the ladder. The latter jumped and landed on the ground with a thud and a new wave of dust swirled around them.

"What do you think, Layton? I feel that this could be the tomb of the last Pharaoh of Egypt," Shohan gave the wall one last prod with the shovel and the entrance crumbled, revealing a pitch-black smaller tunnel.

Layton coughed, waving his hand in front of him. "What? Pharaoh Khai Tutankhamen?"

Shohan nodded, shining an extra torch into the pitch-black darkness.

"Dude, no way I'm going in there. You know I have claustrophobia," Layton said with a hand on his chest.

Shohan laughed, adjusting his helmet light. "Okay, just go back up, I'll shout when I find something."

"No. Wait. Take this with you," Layton handed him a GPS tracker and walkie-talkie. "We don't know if this is safe yet."

"Thanks, Layton," Shohan pocketed the two devices. "You better head up now, don't want you passing out here."

"Good luck, man. Find us some artifacts. Or better, a coffin."

1500 B.C.

Sevrin looked up at the King. Heat rose in his cheeks when he felt the King's eyes roam his entire body with a smirk. He stood up after closing the chest of treasures containing golden statues. He gave the King a quick once-over— he was dressed in the brightest silken kilt tied around his waist; his bronze skin stood out in contrast to the gold bangles around his thick biceps. He had a taut chest decorated with a ruby necklace. His prominent wide shoulders and collar bones were adorned with tattoos of scriptures he did not understand. His headdress with a snakehead ornament intimidated him.

"I apologize, Pharaoh Khai," he said with pride, taking a step forward. "But I am betrothed to the Prince of Saracca," he added with dignity.

Sevrin froze in his spot as the Pharaoh started to stand up from his golden throne. His honey bronzed skin glimmered and he swallowed thickly when he bowed his head and caught sight of the Pharaoh's muscular thigh exposed from the side slit of his silken kilt.

"He may be the Prince of Saracca, but I, am the King of Egypt." The Pharaoh said smugly as he slowly sauntered down the few flights of stairs towards them. "My, my, you may have been the rarest gem I've ever seen across lands and oceans," the Pharaoh, Khai, spoke. His authoritative voice sent shivers down his spine.

"I apologize, King Sejong and Prince Sevrin," he heard the Queen Mother speak, and when she stood near him again, Sevrin could smell the faint hint of Elderflowers. Sevrin wasn't surprised, the Egyptians took pride in their scented oils so it's not an exception that the Queen Mother might own a boudoir of exquisite fine oils. "Akman! Show the King and Prince of Warania to their chambers," the Queen Mother ordered and a servant arrived with a bowed head. "Join us in the Great Hall for dinner, in the meantime, please get some respite."

With that, Sevrin and his father followed the servant named Akman to their assorted chambers.

Sevrin saw chambermaids busying themselves in and out of the other bedchambers. The Pharaoh, King Khai, must have invited royalties across lands, he thought. Sevrin would be lying if he said he didn't feel his heart flutter when the Pharaoh called him a rare gem.

"Son. I was thinking," his father said after he dismissed Akman. "What do you think of calling off the wedding with the Prince of Saracca?"

Sevrin turned and glared at his father. "We had agreements, Father. My marriage with Prince Soho of Saracca will increase our military's forces and neighbouring lands' allies."

"But if you were to marry the Pharaoh, the King of Egypt, we will gain allies from across lands and oceans," his father said nonchalantly.

"Father," Sevrin crossed his arms in front of his chest. "Did you not see how he saw me as an item? A rare gem as he had put it."

"The Prince of Saracca is the fifth in line to the throne. But Pharaoh Khai, he is the King." His father argued.

Sevrin laid down on his bed, groaning in frustration. "I don't want to talk about this right now, father. And I am not hungry, I will not join you at the Great Hall for dinner."

Back in the throne room, Khai continued to receive guests — royalties and nobles who had come from lands far away, bearing gifts and offering their daughters' hand in marriage. However, none interested him since he laid eyes on the Prince of Warania.

CHAPTER 2

Present Day

The sweltering heat of the desert air made it hard to breathe. He crouched as he walked through the narrow tunnel, he had lost count of the number of turns he took. As he ventured further, and probably lower into the ground, the temperature gradually dipped.

A pile of stones blocked another entryway and he began to remove them one by one. An hour passed and he began to see a new entrance. Once the stones were more or less removed and tossed along the narrow tunnelway, he switched on his flashlight and gasped.

Walls were carved with ancient Egyptian scriptures— sacred texts containing pictures of birds, animals, and men themselves. He let his hand trace along one of the first few visible scriptures his torchlight shone.

"The Great Pharaoh, the Golden King."

He read the scriptures, fingers tracing along the well carved-out lines.

He had studied intensively and was well versed in Egyptology. Having uncovered other tombs in Giza with his team, he had the opportunity to translate these hieratic writings and scriptures into modern language.

He set out further with his torch and was mesmerized by the paintings of Egyptian Gods and Deities.

"He treasured gold. He treasured rare gems."

He read in his head.

His team never knew about his obsession with the last King of Egypt. He had spent years digging up research papers from senior Archaeologists, Egyptologists and spent countless nights in libraries with the world's most renowned Historians too. Many have told him that it was impossible to uncover the tomb of the last King of Egypt, that it may have already been emptied by tomb raiders in antiquity, but today, he held onto high hopes.

Pharaoh Khai, as he had read from the numerous published books about the late King, loved gold, he loved treasures and he was said to be buried in his tomb along with his most prized and treasured items.

"During his reign, the city blossomed. People worshipped their King. The King will join his forefathers, along with the Gods and Deities and He will continue to rule Egypt in the underworld."

The senior archaeologist knew the hieroglyphs carved at the most exterior parts of the tomb were words of the priests, words from the people he ruled. What interested him most would be the scriptures in the burial chamber, where generations of Pharaohs started building their Pyramids in their early reigning years before their deaths, leading to the burial chamber. There, would be the scriptures from the King himself.

Except, in the case of Pharaoh Khai Tutankhamen, there was no pyramid. He was said to be buried in the Valley of the Kings, a place far from the pyramids, far from the prying eyes of tomb raiders because the late King did not want his buried treasures to be robbed after his death. However, he needed more concrete information as to whether this was really the last King of Egypt, the final reigning Pharaoh.

The young archaeologist set forth further into the tomb. Some of the paintings have deteriorated and fallen off the walls over the thousands of years it was left standing, hieroglyphs continued all the way down to the furthest end. He shone his torch into the dark abyss— another entrance leading to yet another chamber.

It was filled with gold pleated items— statues of cat-like goddesses, life-size golden sphinxes with the head of a king and a body of a lion, chairs, tables and all sort of furniture painted in gold, laid strewn across the room but one caught the archaeologist's eyes, the first puzzle piece which led him to believe that this could be the tomb of the last King of Egypt, Pharaoh Khai.

On a very corner of the room, laid a small chair, or rather, a throne. It had gold painted on it with rubies embedded in them. He gasped, connecting the dots in his head— Pharaoh Khai had ascended the throne at nine years old when his father passed away unexpectedly which his team of researchers were still finding out till this day. So, he wouldn't be surprised that it was the young Pharaoh who might have sat on this very small golden throne.

"The last Pharaoh of Egypt," he exhaled shakily, smiling nervously to himself as he shone his torch and continued towards the other chambers.

1500 B.C.

Sevrin remained in his chamber after his father left for the Great Hall.

His father's words kept repeating in his head. *The Prince of Saracca is the fifth in line to the throne. But Pharaoh Khai, he is the King.*

Sevrin did not want to disappoint his father. He had grudgingly agreed to the arranged marriage with the Prince of Saracca. He remembered the disappointed look in his mother's eyes when he first told his parents he did not want to marry that young, he was only sixteen. His brother was to be the next King of Warania and so, Sevrin always felt like a spare pawn. But he managed to negotiate the terms with his father that he would only marry the prince after he turned twenty-one years old.

He shook his head. He needed to catch some fresh air.

As he walked out of his chamber archway, two Egyptian guards with spears bowed their heads. Sevrin paid them no mind. He decided to explore the palace.

Sevrin did not know where he was going. He made turns; he went down flights of stoned stairs. He was mesmerized. Back in Warania, their castle was made of black bricks, cement, and gates were made of the strongest wrought iron. But here in Egypt, the palace was mainly made out of limestone, granites, marbles, and possibly clay. What surprised him the most, was there were no doors, only archways. He wondered how the Pharaoh kept his privacy when anyone could enter anywhere and anytime.

Sevrin came upon a darker hallway, it had an archway at the furthest end. With cautious steps, he slowly made his way towards the dark chamber.

He gasped when a pair of ivory eyes stared back at him. They were not human. The eyes glowered in the dark and he thought he heard a soft purr. Curiosity got the better of him as he took a couple of steps closer. With a hand resting on the frame of the archway, he poked his head into the darkness, the same pair of glowing ivory eyes narrowed at him before he heard a loud guttural growl and the sound of heavy chains dragging across the stone floor.

The young prince fell back and sat on the floor, gasping and staring up dumbfounded at the creature that stood so majestically above him. His heart was beating wildly in his chest. It was a cheetah.

"Jafaar!"

Sevrin was too dumbstruck to pay attention to the familiar voice. Before he could even process the fact that a wild cheetah was standing before him, he felt a pair of strong arms wrapped around his waist and hoisted him up on his feet.

"Are you okay, my Prince?"

Sevrin then turned to the voice. It was the Pharaoh, Khai.

"You have a cheetah." He blindly stated, staring blankly at the Pharaoh, he had not fully processed it yet.

"I am aware," Pharaoh Khai only smirked at him before reaching into a sash that was tied around his silken kilt. He fished out a few blocks of raw meat and held his palm up to the wild beast.

Sevrin watched as the cheetah that stood almost as tall as him, gave Pharaoh Khai's hand a curious sniff before he opened his majestic jaws and swallowed the meat hungrily.

"You can pet him, he won't bite," Khai said to the prince who gaped at him in horror. "He won't, not with me around," he reassured with a smile.

Sevrin's heart fluttered when the Pharaoh spoke to him in such a delicate voice and his smile revealed a one-sided dimple. He swallowed nervously when he felt the King reaching down to grab his hand and placed it on top of the cheetah's head.

He let out a shaky breath when the cheetah purred under his touch. "He is so beautiful," Sevrin rasped, his heart still beating wildly in his chest from the close attack earlier. His dainty fingers were trembling but he soon found the confidence and reached further back to pet the feline's fur. "OH—" he gasped, falling a step back when he felt the cheetah lunge forward to rub its head under his chin. The cheetah gave him an experimental lick on the cheek and he let out a muffled chuckle.

Khai's heart leaped, watching the young Prince smile. He would be lying if he said his heart wasn't hammering wildly in his chest when he grabbed the prince's hand. His skin was smooth and soft. Now the Prince's laughter did nothing to calm his already erratic heart. He was telling the truth back in the throne room when he said the young Prince was the rarest gem he had ever laid eyes on. He was the most beautiful person Khai had ever seen, his soft and smooth pale skin, his exotic body chains beneath the robe, the way his eyes crinkled up into crescents when he smiled.

"He likes you," Khai chimed after watching the two's interaction. "Jafaar doesn't warm up to people that easily."

The young Prince turned and smiled at him before returning his attention to his feline pet. "Jafaar. You're a good boy," the Prince, Sevrin, said.

"I didn't see you at the Great Hall. Are you, perhaps, unwell?" Khai asked as he watched Jafaar giving the prince another purr when the latter scratched its favourite spot behind its ear.

Sevrin looked at the Pharaoh, his expression lined with concern and it warmed his chest to know that he cared that much about him. "I just have no appetite."

Khai licked his lips worriedly and nodded. "I'll send a physician to your chamber tonight. I know the sweltering heat and humidity of the desert of Egypt is new to Waranians."

Sevrin fell a step back when Jafaar stood on its hind legs and placed his big paws on his chest, but the Pharaoh was quick to grab the chain around the cheetah's neck and place a hand at the small of his back, stabilizing him. Sevrin blushed when he felt the warmth of his hand seep through his silken robe. He gnawed on his inner cheek as he watched the Pharaoh's toned and bronzed biceps flex when he pulled Jafaar back on all four paws.

"Have you… have you been to Warania?" Sevrin asked shyly, looking at Jafaar who was licking its front paw.

"I have not. But I have heard its daylights are short and it is mostly winter," Khai said, handing Jafaar another cube of raw meat to distract it when it tried to leap towards the prince's direction.

Sevrin only nodded. He tried to not ogle the way the Pharaoh's exposed chest and abdominal muscles flexed with every pull of the cheetah's chain. He only hoped the King had not spotted his reddened ears and cheeks.

Khai let out a breathy chuckle. "I know you said you have no appetite. But our cook makes the best potato stew. It's good to warm up your stomach before you sleep tonight," Khai threw a few cubes of raw meat into the cheetah's dark chamber and the feline leaped into the abyss. "The desert gets cold when night falls."

With a shy nod, Sevrin followed the Pharaoh towards the Great Hall. He had his heart in his mouth the entire way up, he felt nervous around the King but he also felt a strange pull of attraction towards him.

Present day

He ventured into multiple chambers with similar settings — hieratic writings, paintings of the Gods, sacred texts, and scriptures lining the limestone walls. He was enamoured, of how in ancient times, people have skilfully carved out these writings so beautifully, it felt almost magical. These chambers were also packed with gold items. There were also chests that could not be opened by his bare hands, bows and arrows that seemed to have been made by the highest quality of ivory back then, and golden tankards of various shapes with a plethora of jewels embedded on them. This tomb was unusually lavish. It showed the opulence and power the Pharaoh had.

On one side of the limestone wall, a vast painting with its colours still mostly intact, depicted a King standing on a golden chariot with his warhorse on its hindlegs, behind him was his army of soldiers holding bows with arrows, others had spears.

What captivated the young archaeologist was that amongst the Egyptian soldiers behind the Pharaoh, there were also soldiers who were dressed in an entirely different raiment. Could the Pharaoh have gone to war with his allies? If so, what had caused the war?

"He was not just a King. He was a great warrior, a respected General."

The hieroglyphs continued down every wall. Not a single piece of stone was left uncarved.

"While his forefathers had over a hundred wives and bore descendants as abundant as the stars, the King, had no heir."

He entered another chamber. The walls were twice as high, the room twice as large. He shone his torch against the walls and something new caught his eyes— other than paintings and carved scriptures, there were wooden fire torches built on each corner of all four walls, its wooden stave had splintered over the centuries, the cloth wrapped on its end looked burnt. The Pharaoh must have spent a great amount of time building his burial chamber.

"He had the power of a King and the virility of a lion."

He took a couple of steps back to admire the paintings on the walls and his back hit on something solid. Rubbing soothing circles on the dimple of his spine, he turned and shone his light at the obstacle he had bumped into, only to gape in shock.

A coffin. A solid gold coffin— its head was adorned with a headdress, its blue-golden-striped which mimicked a cloth, fell to its shoulders, a centrepiece snakehead ornament decorating the crown. He dusted off part of the coffin and he could almost see his reflection through the gold.

He ran his fingers along the golden coffin and began reading the scriptures carved at its perimeter. Specifically, he was looking for a special symbol that could spell out the Pharaoh's name— a cartouche, an oval-shaped symbol that encapsulated a royal member's name.

"The great ruler of Egypt. The last King who reigned in the Middle Empire. The Divine King who is now one with the Gods and Deities."

His heart leaped when he found the cartouche carved beautifully beside those hieroglyphs.

"Pharaoh Khai Tutankhamen."

CHAPTER 3

1500 B.C.

Back in his chamber, Sevrin laid on his featherbed as an Egyptian physician attended to him. He had a bronze bowl filled with water and a single basil leaf.

The physician lightly placed two fingers on the pulse point of his wrist.

His father stood by his side, concern lining his thick brows. He ran his calloused fingers through his beard and Sevrin knew his father was getting impatient.

The priest closed his eyes, chanting a spell, two fingers held up between his brow bone. *"Niakas shahkzwan thebesnas sonnus goddowath."* The priest chanted softly and Sevrin jolted lightly when he took the drenched basil leaf and started swatting water at his face.

"Is he alright?" He heard his father say after the priest stood up, collecting his bronze bowl of what he thought would be holy water. The Egyptians were known to be religious. Even though Sevrin felt slightly uncomfortable with the priest's unusual ritual, he did not show his displeasure.

The Egyptian priest bowed slightly. "The prince shall be well after catching some respite. It is nothing worrisome, Your Highness."

His father nodded. "Thank you. You are dismissed. Please give our regards to the Pharaoh."

The priest bowed once more. "Yes, Your Highness." With that, he retreated a few steps backward, head still slightly bowed before he straightened and walked out of their chamber.

Sevrin sat up on his featherbed, wiping his face with the sleeve of his robe.

His father sat beside him, resting a palm on his cheek. "I'm sending a missive to the King of Saracca at first light."

"What do you mean? We are only here for the Pharaoh's birthday. It won't be long till we are set to go back," Sevrin scooted closer to his father. He had an uneasy gut feeling about this. "We'd pass by Saracca on our way home." He protested.

King Sejong took a deep breath and forced out a smile. "I have seen how the Pharaoh cared about you tonight. When you weren't there at the Great Hall, he had looked forlorn, worried if I may say. His eyes kept looking back to the empty seat next to mine."

Sevrin's heart swelled at that thought.

"Princesses from other Kingdoms offered to have a dance

with the Pharaoh, he all but rejected them before he left the Great Hall, saying he had to feed his pet." His father reached down and cupped Sevrin's hand in both of his. "But the Pharaoh was gleaming when he re-entered the Great Hall with you. The ambiance was lifted at your presence. And now he even had a physician sent up for you."

Sevrin remembered Pharaoh Khai's smile when he was petting Jafaar. He didn't know he had that much impact on the King.

"I know you will be in the Pharaoh's good hands. Egypt may be far from Warania, but knowing that he will treat you well and respectfully, brings peace to my mind." His father almost sobbed at the end and it pained his heart.

Sevrin had lived under his father and brother's protection back in their castle in Warania. Everywhere he went, he always had one of his family members by his side. It scared him that his father wished to marry him off far away from his homeland. It even took a week for them to travel here in Egypt by horse carriages.

"I'm calling off the wedding with the Prince of Saracca."

"Father," Sevrin reached out and wrapped his arms around his father's broad chest, his rough beard nuzzling his forehead. "I don't want to leave you. Egypt is too far away…" he started sobbing but his father only patted him on his head.

"Do you, perhaps, not fancy the King?" His father pried the sobbing prince off his chest and wiped away the tears with his calloused thumbs.

Sevrin dipped his head. He could feel a slight heat creeping up his neck. "I would say the Pharaoh is thoughtful."

His father grinned. "That's at least something, isn't it, my boy?"

"But…" Sevrin protested, remembering the female royalty who sat beside the Pharaoh during dinner at the great hall. "The Pharaoh is married to the Princess of Begonia. If I marry him, I will be…" he trailed off, the sudden thought of coming in second to someone else stirred jealousy in the pit of his stomach.

"Princess Nari has been married to the Pharaoh for three years. Yet she had not produced him an heir. And the King himself have not proclaimed her to be his rightful Queen." His father reassured.

Sevrin kept mum. He knew he could never talk his father out of it. Everything since his birth was planned by his father.

When Sevrin didn't speak, his father pulled the eiderdowns over him. "You know I am just a missive away. Warania will still be your home regardless of where you are."

Sevrin nodded. He laid back down and flipped on his side. Closing his eyes, he replayed the scene of him with the Pharaoh and his pet cheetah, Jafaar.

Khai had been kept busy by the royal court and political officials in his study the past three days. He had felt guilty for not being there to entertain his guests who had travelled weeks here for his birthday. More specifically, he had missed seeing the young Prince of Warania.

"The Nile River had dried up for the past year and a half," Plato, his royal advisor, said with a respectful bow of his head. "Farmers have lost their crops, the people of Egypt will go into famine."

Khai rested his elbows on his gold pleated table, massaging his temples with his hands. The River of Nile that flooded yearly had blessed their soil with crops for centuries. This was the first time a major drought had happened. "Ration out five hundred sacks of rice and potatoes to the people."

"My King," another court official, Ptolem, came forward. "We can't keep rationing out stocks to the people. Something has to be done."

"Ptolem is right, Pharaoh Khai," said Agafya, the royal astrologist. "The Gods have been angered by the sins of the living. A sacrifice must be made by the King, then the Nile river shall flood once more and fertilize our soil."

"A sacrifice will take several moons to prepare, my people are starving, there is no time for a sacrifice," Khai asserted, rubbing his palm up and down his face tiredly. He had been cooped up in his study with court officials bugging him with royal duties for days and he needed to blow off some steam.

The priest who he had personally sent up to the prince's chamber stepped forward. "If I may, my King," the priest looked up at him for permission to continue.

Khai was surprised, the priest usually kept to himself, but seeing how he had stepped forward, he must have a plan. He nodded and gestured for the priest to continue.

"The Gods have blessed the King with a wife but have yet to produce an heir." The priest stated, hands held together.

Khai sighed in frustration. He saw Plato, his royal advisor, throwing the priest a warning glare. If anyone were to come at him again for not having an heir, he swore he would rearrange the royal court members himself.

"Maybe our King needs to have a second marriage instead of a sacrifice?"

A chorus of whispers echoed around his study chamber. Khai hummed in thought as he watched some of his court officials nodding and exchanging comments of the priest's suggestion.

"Princesses and Princes from Kingdoms across lands have gathered here for a special occasion," Plato stepped forward once more. "And since the Festival of the Sun God Ra is just a few days away, it would be a good opportunity to seek one of the King's daughters or sons for their hand in marria—"

"A missive for King Sejong from the King of Saracca." A commanding soldier who guarded the main entrance of the palace barged in before his royal advisor could finish his sentence.

Khai then dismissed his court and his royal officials filed out without another word.

"Send for King Sejong in my study." Khai took the rolled scroll from his guard. "I'll give this to him personally."

"Yes, my King."

Sevrin woke up to an empty chamber. His father was not around. His father's personal royal guard was not outside of their chamber either. He must have accompanied his father somewhere.

He was donning his body chain when he saw his father walk into their chamber with a missive in his hand. He was gleaming and his father rarely looked this happy.

"The King of Saracca had sent word, I had just met with the Pharaoh. He said he will be asking for your hand in marriage personally."

Sevrin slipped the barbell of his body chain through his navel piercing. He held his breath.

"The Saraccan King gives his blessings but still wishes to tie our allies."

Sevrin felt guilty upon hearing that. He was only sixteen when his parents made an agreement with the King of Saracca that he would marry their Prince when he turned twenty-one. Now at twenty years old, his father had called off the wedding. He wondered if he would have felt anything towards the prince if he had met him. Maybe, if he hadn't joined his father here in Egypt, he would still be marrying the prince.

With a sigh, he grabbed his robe and sat on the featherbed. "Would the King and Prince think ill of me?"

King Sejong strode towards his son, taking a seat beside him. "If they had thought that way, they wouldn't be sending their blessings. They would have sent an army marching towards Warania."

Sevrin dipped his head.

His father spoke when he kept silent. "Alright. Dress up now. The Pharaoh is expecting you in his study chamber."

The prince brightened at that and his heart leaped. He had not seen the Pharaoh for the past three days. He had not dared to venture back into the dark hallway either. He wouldn't want to be mauled by the wild beast. He didn't remember how to get there anyway.

One of the Egyptian guards saw the wandering Prince and guided him to the Pharaoh's study.

"Thank you." Sevrin dismissed the guard.

Standing at the front of the archway of the Pharaoh's study, with two guards holding spears that intimidated him, he swallowed nervously and forced his legs to carry him forward.

"Pharaoh Khai." The prince spotted the King behind his golden table, carving scriptures onto what seemed like clay.

The King's study was bigger than their guest chamber. High ceilings were painted with the images of Gods and Deities, walls were chiselled with Egyptian scriptures, it looked like a temple of its own.

"My Prince!" The pharaoh dropped his carving tools and stood up, eyes glimmering as he smiled at him.

Sevrin stayed rooted in his spot. He still felt nervous around the King. "You wanted to see me, Pharaoh Khai?" His voice came out soft and shaky and he cringed inwardly at how unconfident he sounded for a prince.

"I'm sure King Sejong had told you?" The Pharaoh slowly walked down the three flights of steps, making his way towards the prince.

Sevrin only nodded. His heart hammered when he made eye contact with the Pharaoh and he quickly dipped his head.

Pharaoh Khai stood in front of him and he could feel the warm heat the King was emitting. The Pharaoh had donned a beige kilt today, red sash tied around his waist and instead of the ruby necklace he last saw the King wore, he had a golden necklet clasped around his neck with scriptures carved around it. Sevrin wished he knew what the writings meant.

Sevrin quickly looked up, not wanting to stare at the Pharaoh's taut chest and his chiselled abs. He was then met with his kohl-lined eyes.

"I had wanted to ask you personally," the Pharaoh explained, his voice authoritative but sounded just as delicate.

Sevrin licked his lips nervously and he saw the King's gaze darted down to his lips for a second. He blushed.

"This will be my second marriage. But for you, my Prince, this will be your first," Pharaoh Khai paused as if to gauge the prince's expression. "I want this to feel special to you as it will be to me. My father never had another extravagant wedding with his other wives after my mother. But I want to do things right with you."

Sevrin let out a breath he did not know he was holding.

"Will you marry me, Prince Sevrin?" The Pharaoh held up his palm.

Sevrin had thought that Pharaoh Khai had wanted to claim him since he first bore gifts to the King during his birthday at the throne room. A rare gem as he had said. If the King had seen him as a prized item, he would not have done this. His heart swelled as he broke into a faint smile.

Holding out his hand to place it on the Pharaoh's opened palm, and with a soft voice, he said, "I do."

CHAPTER 4

1500 B.C.

Dancers, acrobats, magicians, and many more kept the Pharaoh and his guests entertained as they dined. Pharaoh Khai and Princess Nari were seated at the centre with their very own private table with two guest tables lining each side.

Sevrin caught Pharaoh Khai glancing at him several times. He didn't dare to smile or look in his direction. Princess Nari who sat beside the King, had glared at him the first time he looked at the Pharaoh longer than he should. She had similar kohl-lined eyes and it looked intimidating. She also had gold earrings that hung down to her shoulders. The gold necklace and bangles she wore, glimmered. However, she did not have a headdress as a Queen would.

As they dined on, Sevrin felt more nervous. When the last performance was dismissed, he saw Pharaoh Khai stand up from his golden throne.

"I would like to apologize for my absence the past couple of days," Khai said with a chalice of wine held on one hand. "To make up for the lost time, since the festival of the Sun God Ra is nearing, I would love to invite all of you to Karnak Temple. There, the Sun God Ra will bless you with health, love, fertility, luck, and riches."

Nods went around the hall. Princesses jumped in their seats in excitement. Everyone wanted to explore the walls beyond the palace.

"I will have sedans and horses arranged for all of you. It would be an honour to have all the Great Kings of this realm to journey with me to the high temple."

Kings smiled and their Princes beamed with pride. Egypt was known to have the most glamorous temples where only pure-blooded royalties and dedicated high priests could set foot there. Rumours that travelled across lands had also said that prayers in the Karnak Temple rarely go unanswered.

However, Sevrin and his father were never religious. They did not believe in life after death.

His heart hammered in his chest when the Pharaoh looked his way.

"I would also like to announce that in the high temple of Karnak, I will wed the young Prince of Warania."

All heads turned to him and he felt his cheeks flushed with heat. He briefly glanced at Princess Nari, her eyes seethed with rage when the Pharaoh left his throne and sauntered to his side.

"Prince Sevrin of Warania and I," Pharaoh Khai offered his palm out and Sevrin placed his trembling hand on his and stood up. "Will be wedded on the day of the Festival of Sun God Ra. We would like to have the Kings' blessings."

Princesses who came to Egypt with hopes of marrying the Pharaoh were dismayed, though they gave them their blessings.

Khai and the young prince stayed till all the other royalties had left for their chambers for the night.

"My King."

Khai turned, surprised to see Princess Nari still around.

"Shall I see you at your chambers tonight?" Princess Nari said in a low sultry voice, snaking an arm around his waist, her smooth hand lightly placed on his exposed chest.

Khai felt the young Prince's hand loosening on his grip,

attempting to pull away. Khai only grabbed him tighter.

"I will not be in my chambers tonight. I will be seeing my court officials and the high priestesses in my study for the preparation of the wedding. You should rest early, Princess."

Princess Nari threw Sevrin a glare before removing her hands from the Pharaoh. With a bow, she said, "Goodnight, my King."

Khai watched the Princess grudgingly leave the Great Hall with her personally selected group of guards and chambermaids in tow. Servants and cupbearers were starting to clean up the tables.

"Do not mind her, my Prince," Khai, still holding the young Prince's hand firmly, turned slightly to face him.

Sevrin worried his bottom lip, not wanting to meet the Pharaoh's eyes. He felt unwelcome by the Princess but he did not want to concern the King.

"I know this is a rushed ceremony," Khai let his thumb that was holding the prince's hand, rub soothing circles, feeling the soft skin beneath his. "But I will not do anything that will make you uncomfortable, my Prince."

Sevrin's heart did a million somersaults at that.

With a slight hesitation, Khai brought up his free hand, placing his palm against the prince's pale cheek. For the first time, Khai felt things he never knew he could. He wanted to give him all the luxury and comfort, he wanted to protect him, but most of all, he wanted to give the young Prince his heart. "So beautiful," Khai exhaled, letting his palm linger a little longer on the prince's now blushed cheeks.

Sevrin dipped his head although a part of him wanted to lean into his touch. He only hoped the Pharaoh did not hear his wild heart beating in his chest.

Two guards walked into the great hall. Khai recognized them as the guards outside the prince's chamber. He let go of his hand but his heart got caught in his mouth when the Waranian Prince tightened his hold on him.

"Will I see you tomorrow, Pharaoh Khai?"

Khai's smile hung ear to ear. He was happy to know the prince wanted to see him as much as he did. "Yes, my Prince."

Sevrin let go of Pharaoh Khai's hand and joined the guards.

"Goodnight, my Prince." Khai held a hand to his chest, and for the first time, he gave a slight bow.

Servants, chambermaids, kitchen cooks, and all the royal staff were clambering and running about the palace. Everyone was tasked with the wedding preparation.

A royal seamstress held a red string to measure his shoulders, tailoring a robe for the wedding. She cut it into pieces and placed them accordingly in a silken cloth.

Chambermaids then drew up a hot water bath filled with roses and scented oils. Sevrin approached the slightly bowed ladies-in-waiting and opened his arms, allowing them to strip him off of his Waranian royal robe. He thought he caught sight of a few of them blushed when they first saw his body chain.

"You may be dismissed," Sevrin proceeded to slowly step and lower himself into the bath that was just as big as his guest chamber. Aromatic smells of the scented oils mixed with roses wafted through the air and Sevrin submerged himself further into the bath, relaxing his body and letting his head rest on the curb.

"The prince shall have his private chambers just like the Princess," Khai instructed Plato.

They were in Khai's study, with him supervising a craftsman that was engraving a stone head with the announcement of the coming wedding to notify the commoners in the village.

"But, my King, the only chambers left are the guest-chambers."

Khai rounded behind the craftsman and nodded in appreciation at the beautifully engraved writings.

"Empty the West Wing of the palace. There, the Prince shall reside," Khai then proceeded to his royal seamstress with her red measuring string prepared.

Plato looked up at his Pharaoh, dumbfounded. "My King, but the West Wing is where you store your treasured golds and gems, no one was ever allowed to step foot in there."

Khai gave his royal advisor a thoughtful hum. "Throw

them in the Valley of the Kings. I do not need them anymore."

Plato's jaw fell slack, eyes widened. He had never seen his King so nonchalant about his most treasured golds. For a moment, he thought he had heard his King wrongly. "You mean…" he trailed off, not wanting to offend his King.

"Yes, Plato. My burial chamber. I do not care where you toss them." Khai turned for his royal seamstress to measure his collar.

Plato stood firmly on his spot, unable to form a reply.

When Plato didn't speak, Khai turned to fix his royal advisor with a questionable raise of his brow. "What are you waiting for? Make haste!"

"Y-y-yes, my King." Plato, still dumbfounded by his King's turn of attitude for his golds, stuttered and retreated out of his King's study chamber.

Plato, with his short and stubby legs, hurriedly gathered a few servants on his way. "Prepare a few wagons and follow me to the West Wing." He demanded and the servants looked at him with the same surprised expression as he did earlier. "Pharaoh's orders. Now!"

Much to Sevrin's dismay, he did not get to see Pharaoh Khai in all their dinings in the Great Hall the next few days. Princess Nari was not present either. He wondered if the King was still busy with their wedding preparations.

Kings exchanged conversations with other great Kings. Princes offered a hand for a dance with other Princesses from other Kingdoms. Tambourines, lutes, and sistrums resonated in the Great Hall as Princes and Princesses danced and mingled. Sevrin wished the Pharaoh was here. He wanted to dance too.

"It's a shame your mother cannot attend your wedding," his father remarked after sipping his wine.

His mother had been nursing her ailing health for a long time and hence could not travel far outside Warania. He only hoped his mother had been proud of him at least.

"At least she played her last pawn," Sevrin stated and his father only frowned at him.

"Both your mother and I, only want the best for you, Sevrin." His father ruffled his hair before draping his arm over his shoulders, giving them a firm squeeze. "As I said, Warania will forever be your home and we are just a missive away."

Present day

He dusted more dust off the coffin. Standing back to admire the gold casket, he let out an exasperated breath. It was beautiful, intricate, and elegant.

A part of him felt cautious. He had heard myths that Pharaohs' coffin were hexed with spells. He remembered reading a research paper of another young archaeologist who unearthed the very first coffin under one of the pyramids in the sixteenth century— Howard Carter, who had unexpectedly met with an accident just a mere three months after unearthing a Pharaoh's coffin which now resided in Egypt's National Museum of Ancient History.

"It took me so long to find you," he rasped, rounding the golden coffin and letting his fingers trace along those intricate patterns.

Not much of the late Pharaoh Khai was mentioned in the other tombs of previous reigning monarchs. All he knew from his studies, were that the King ascended the throne when he was just a child, helped his father won wars when he was eighteen, and from what he had selectively gathered from the engravings on the limestone walls, Pharaoh Khai was obsessed with golds and rare treasures. But if he did love them, why were his treasured items strewn so carelessly in the other chambers?

He stepped away from the golden coffin and shone his light on the walls.

"The Sun God Ra shall shine when the King, the Divine Pharaoh, rises from the horizon."

Many questions swamped the young archaeologist's mind.

"Even Pharaohs had to live in constant danger and fear from their own families and relatives."

"How did you die?" Shohan whispered to himself, readjusting his spectacles on his nose bridge. "Were you murdered? Or did you die on a battlefield?" He recalled seeing an engraved pictorial of the Pharaoh on his chariot, pulled by his warhorse.

"The Pharaoh, just like the Sun God Ra, will set below the horizon and pass over the riverbank of Nile and go to rest in his eternal home to the west of Khairo."

"Khairo…" Shohan muttered in a hushed voice, as if afraid of awakening what laid inside the coffin. His eyes widened at the realization. The Pharaoh, Khai, must have won wars in his final reigning days. The capital of Egypt must have been named under their Great Pharaoh Khai— Khairo, or in this modern-day, Cairo.

"I can't believe I finally found you," he let out shakily.

He stiffened when he heard a low breathing presence and cautious approaching footsteps.

With his headlight still on, he turned and briefly saw a man before his knees gave way. His helmet fell on the floor and the light died, submerging him in the dark abyss.

"Lay…Layton… is that you?" He shakily exhaled. He could not even see his own hands in this pure darkness. "This isn't funny."

He clambered backwards on his bottom until his back hit a wall. He could hear blood drumming in his ears and his heart was palpitating crazily in his chest. A pair of footsteps grazed the gravel nearby and Shohan swallowed nervously.

He heard a swoosh before the entire chamber lit up. Blinded by the lights momentarily, he held up his elbow to cover his eyes.

Still slightly trembling, the archaeologist slowly lowered his arm, letting his eyes adjust to the blinding brightness. Fire torches were lit and there, standing mighty and tall before him, was a man with tanned skin that glimmered. He had a white kilt tied around his waist, a golden sash wrapped loosely around it. He had the most chiselled abs and taut sternum, collar bones were lined with tattoos of ancient scriptures, golden bangles glistened around his thickly veined wrists and biceps, his neck hung the prettiest and brightest ruby he had ever seen. His jaw was angled and sharp, his eyes were lined with black kohl and he wore a headpiece with striped silken cloth reaching down to his broad shoulders, the same snakehead ornament he had seen on the golden coffin, centered on his crown.

"My prince?"

CHAPTER 5

Present day

Shohan looked at the man dressed in ancient Egyptian attire.

His legs felt wobbly. He wanted to up and run but he could not muster the courage to.

"My beautiful… prince…"

He heard the man speak again. His voice sounded hurt.

Shohan's eyes darted towards the solid gold coffin. The lid was partly shifted open. He did not move it, so it could only mean one thing. The man standing before him was none other than the Pharaoh himself.

The man, no, the *Pharaoh's* expression was lined with pain, his kohl-lined eyes were bloodshot and almost teary.

The archaeologist started hyperventilating. He needed to run. If this truly was the Pharaoh, then the myths were true, that all Pharaohs' coffins were protected with a sorcerer's spell and whoever opened or disturbed the tomb, shall be cursed.

He gathered up all his courage and stood up slowly.

"I have longed to see you again, my dear Prince Sevrin…"

Shohan's lips were trembling with fear. He took a step back when the Pharaoh, in all flesh and glory, slowly approached him, one hand extending out towards him.

He let out a whimper and forced his eyes shut when he felt a warm palm resting against his cheek. The touch was smooth and gentle, it did not seem like the Pharaoh wanted to hurt him.

Was he a ghost? Was he a mummy like he had seen in the movies? Did he possess powers? Was he just a manifestation of the Pharaoh's soul? Or was this all a figment of his imagination for wanting to find Pharaoh Khai Tutankhamen's tomb for so long?

He eyed the archway of the chamber that led to the other rooms of golds and treasures. If he ran fast enough, he could call for Bentley. But would the Pharaoh run after him?

He was starting to feel dizzy by the lack of oxygen from being more than six feet underground for hours now. He needed to run. Without even throwing the Pharaoh one last look, the trembling archaeologist sprinted out of the chamber, he did not look back. All he heard was a gentle whisper, "Don't go, my Prince. Please don't leave me again."

He ran and ran. His back felt exposed, it felt like he could be sucked back into the burial chamber and he was terrified out of his wits.

He panted as he climbed up the ladder.

"Dude."

He heard his junior intern, Bentley, said. He turned and looked back down into the dark tunnel. He wasn't being followed.

"Dude you look like you've seen a ghost," Bentley raised a brow at him as he sipped on a packet of juice. "Found anything?"

Should he tell Bentley? Would they think he had finally gone dipshit crazy? He shook his head, wiping sweat away from his forehead. That was also when he realized he had left his spectacles in the burial chamber when he fell. "No," he lied, "just plain stones and rubbles and tunnelways."

Bentley nodded. "Well, anyway, the team got a call from Dr. Jaime. Looks like they found something in their aerial seismic scan not far from here. Dr. Layton had left to excavate with the team there."

Shohan's head was still muddled from the encounter with the dead Pharaoh's manifestation. But was it a manifestation? He had felt the Pharaoh's warm hand. It felt real.

He held up his hand and cupped a side of his cheek where the Pharaoh had touched.

"Hey, you okay? Dr. Shohan?" Bentley waved a hand in front of his face.

"Uh?"

"I was saying, do you want to abandon this hopeless tomb and join up with our team?"

He couldn't make up his mind. He was sure the strewn gold treasures and the solid gold coffin he saw and touched were not made up in his head. He had felt the intricate design of the golden coffin and the beautifully engraved scriptures with his very own hands.

1500 B.C.

Sevrin stepped out of his bathing chamber and his ladies-in-waiting dried him off. He proceeded to his chest of jewelleries and picked a new set of body chain, this time with quartz decorating his navel barbell.

His seamstress arrived holding out a white robe with a silvery sheen. He stepped into the robe and the seamstress tied the silken robe around his waist before ending with a firm knot over his right shoulder. The robe fell over his knees, his left shoulder was left exposed but kept his body chain hidden well underneath. The seamstress slipped him a pair of golden sandals before securing his waist with a golden sash just like he saw on Pharaoh Khai in his study when he proposed.

Chambermaids dusted his cheekbones with rogues of gold, lined his eyes with black kohl, and styled his hair with rose oil. They ground rose petals into fine dust, mixing it with oil before lightly dabbing his soft lips with it. They also crowned his head with a garland of peony and stephanotis.

The royal seamstress re-entered his chamber and presented a veil to him.

"The Pharaoh requested Your Highness to wear this." The seamstress proceeded to hook the chains on both sides of his ears. The veil covered his lower face, it felt soft against his skin and it smelled of lavender which calmed his nerves.

Guards with spears outside his chamber ushered him to the throne room.

The Pharaoh, Khai, was donned in a yellow-gold kilt with silver sash, his snakehead ornamented headpiece with blue-and-gold striped silk cloth rested over his shoulders. He was also holding a cane with a Sphinx decorating the handle. Gold bangles and ruby necklace stood out in contrast to his dark skin that glimmered with a sheen of gold dust.

"My Prince, you look beautiful..." Khai exhaled, eyes only for the Waranian Prince that will soon become his husband. He caught a whiff of his perfume oil; it was light but alluring and it almost made his head spin.

Sevrin blushed and he was glad he had a face veil on.

"Thank you, Pharaoh Khai," he said with a bow.

Khai held his hand out and when the young Prince took hold of his hand, he felt every nerve sparked in his body as he guided him to his sedan.

Sevrin let go of the Pharaoh's hand after he sat on his richly decorated sedan chair. It also had a canopy over his head to protect him from the harsh desert sun.

"Sit tight, my beautiful Prince," Khai reached up to the canopy and pulled off the strings and silken curtains rolled down to the floor on all four sides of the sedan, covering the prince.

With Khai's command, guards on all four corners of the sedan lifted it up by their poles, resting them on their shoulders.

They started their journey towards the high temple of Karnak.

Sevrin's hands were cold and clammy but he eventually trusted the guards that were lifting his sedan. The silken curtains were partly see-through and he could see fan bearers walking on both sides of his sedan.

Khai rode on his black warhorse with the prince's sedan following behind him. Royal guards on horses preceded at the front, making sure commoners stayed behind their line while some guards strode along the sides with spears, ready to jump into attack if any of the royal members came under assassination.

Royal Kings including King Sejong, Princes, and Princesses in both sedans and horses followed closely behind the Waranian Prince, waving to the commoners.

A procession of drummers and trumpeters marched behind with the Royal Egyptian military forces, playing their music to announce the royal wedding of the Pharaoh.

Servants were at the last of the marching line, rowing barrels and wagons full of offerings that were to be used during the wedding ceremony in the high temple.

Sevrin watched through his curtains— commoners dressed in tunics, some in rags, hooted and waved at the approaching Pharaoh and his sedan. Everyone wanted a glimpse of the Waranian Prince. Villagers held up garlands of white roses with their palms pressed together to show their respect to their Pharaoh. Some even threw rice over them to bless their King.

Khai looked over and saw a little boy coming a little too close to the approaching sedan. A light breeze swept by, causing the silken curtains to part open, slightly revealing the prince. What caught his heart, was watching his fiancé's pale hand reaching out through the slit of the silken curtains to receive a white rose from the little boy dressed in rags.

In his sedan, Sevrin gave the little boy a wave and his heart leaped when the boy squealed and jumped in his mother's arms.

More people wanted to have a first-hand interaction with the prince after witnessing the exchange with the boy in rags. Egyptian guards with spears tightened their security around the sedan, making sure no one else came closer.

Music from the royal musicians, the hurrahs and hails of the villagers drummed in his ears. The hot sun and humidity of the desert made his throat parched. As they neared the high temple of Karnak, the boisterous sound of villagers slowly dwindled, save for the royal musicians marching behind.

Sevrin tightly gripped onto the armrest of his sedan when the guards lowered him to the ground. An approaching figure pushed aside the front curtains of his sedan. The Pharaoh reached out a hand while his other held the curtain open for him to step out.

Khai held onto the prince's hand, leading him out. The commoners cheered when they spotted the Pharaoh's new prince from afar.

Sevrin shyly gave the people a small wave before he was led by Pharaoh Khai towards the entrance of Karnak Temple. Other royalties followed right behind them and he could hear gasps from Princesses as they admired the temple's architecture.

The music never stopped even when they set foot on the temple's holy ground. Both sides of the temple were lined with stone statues of sphinxes that stood as tall as men. High priests awaited at the doors of the temple for Sevrin and the Pharaoh.

Royal musicians and guards stood outside the temple. Wheels and barrels were rolled into the temple's courtyard while servants proceeded to prepare for the evening feast.

The high priest of the temple received a pair of cranes from a servant at the door of the temple.

"May the Gods and Deities receive the news of the procession of the royal wedding." The high priest swatted holy water at the cranes with a single basil leaf before setting the cranes free. The pair of cranes flew into the late afternoon sky, wings soaring majestically before disappearing beyond the horizon.

"You may enter, Your Majesties." The high priest stepped aside and bowed his head, holding the door open for the Pharaoh and his Prince.

With Pharaoh Khai never once letting go of his hand, they walked towards another group of priestesses. The temple was enormous, the paintings on the well-carved high ceiling magnified its grandeur. Small squared window shafts situated on the walls allowed silver rays of sunlight into the temple.

Sevrin was befuddled. He was never a religious person and so, the entire ritual was new to him. He followed whatever the Pharaoh was doing.

Royalties invited to their wedding were seated behind them as both men knelt on a feather cushion.

Khai chuckled seeing his Prince fumbling with every movement, he pressed his palms together and watched the young prince follow suit.

A high priest approached them with a red string. "May the sky, where our Gods reside, open their gates for the Deities to join in the procession of the royal wedding of the Great Pharaoh of Egypt," the priest tied the red string on Sevrin's wrist and extended it towards the Pharaoh. "And May the Sun God Ra shine over the horizon of the Valley of the Kings to awaken the great monarchs that now ruled the netherworld," the priest chanted and tied the same red string over the Pharaoh's wrist.

The same priest returned with his decanter of myrrh oil. "The Gods shall anoint the Great King of Egypt, Pharaoh Khai," he dribbled a small amount onto the King's palm and proceeded to do the same with the prince. "And the young Prince Sevrin of Warania, as one."

A new priest came forward from behind the altar with a burning sage incense. He circled Sevrin and the Pharaoh, muttering chants of blessing, the smoke of the incense created a grey circle around them. "With the blessings of the Gods and Deities, I now pronounce you as husbands."

Claps and cheers from the royal families, relatives, and friends reverberated around the temple hall while the same high priest who anointed them with oil, came forward to untie the red string that tied their wrists.

Another younger priest with a bald head came forward with a golden bowl of holy water. Sevrin watched Pharaoh Khai, now his husband, rinse his hands in the water and he followed suit.

Sevrin was almost relieved that he could now stand after kneeling for so long. He felt a strong grip on his forearm. Pharaoh Khai had helped him up.

Khai took hold of both his Prince's hands, facing him. He lifted the face veil slightly and leaned in. He felt the prince tensed and so he hesitated and instead, he placed a soft kiss on the prince's cheek.

Sevrin's heart was almost hammering out of his chest. He had never kissed anyone. He didn't know how to either. So when the Pharaoh leaned in, he had panicked. Now he only hoped he had not disappointed his husband. Part of him wanted to kiss him too.

Khai, with his hand still firmly grabbing his Prince, turned, and announced to the other royalties gathered to witness the union of their wedding. "Let the feast begin!"

Sevrin and his Pharaoh dined on their own separate table at the temple's courtyard that was filled with a plethora of fruit baskets, fowls, rice, wine, and many more. Kings and Princes from other kingdoms began to toast to the newlyweds.

The spiced wine left a bitter taste on his tongue and it heated his chest and stomach. Sevrin had never had such strong wine, it almost burned his throat. More Kings and Princes took turns toasting to him and his Pharaoh. By the time Sevrin had his fifteenth drink, his head was almost spinning.

Khai was starting to get worried for his Prince. As the King of Wicklow continued to congratulate him while trying his luck to push his daughter into a third marriage with him, he saw the young Prince holding his cup up for the King of Kattergar to pour him some wine. The prince had missed and the wine spilled on the table.

"I'll drink on his behalf," Khai raised his wine cup to the King of Kattergar who nodded in understanding.

"Thank you everyone for spending your time here in the

Temple of Karnak," Khai stood up, gathering the attention of all the royalties present. "Me and my Prince feel honoured to have the blessings from the great Kings across this realm."

Sevrin planted his elbow on the table as he rested one side of his cheek on his palm. The Pharaoh continued to give his speech but he couldn't decipher anymore. His head was spinning and he felt slightly nauseous. He heard more cheers, more applause before he felt a hand wrapped around his wrist. He looked up to see Pharaoh Khai.

"My Prince, it's time to leave."

He let himself be pulled up by the Pharaoh. He stumbled a bit as they made their way towards the entrance of the temple. He heard people talking but he couldn't make out who. All he knew was that he wanted to sleep.

"Guards."

"Yes, my King."

"Get my horse."

"What about the Prince's seda—"

"It's not safe when he's drunk. He will ride with me."

"Yes, my King."

Sevrin did not know how he even got onto the horse. He felt unsteady until a strong arm wrapped around his waist while the other held onto the bridle of the horse.

Pharaoh Khai tightened his grip on his Prince's waist as their horse started strutting out of the temple with a perimeter of guards holding spears on horses surrounding them.

The ride was uncomfortable. Sevrin kept lolling his head and every time he did, the arm around his waist tightened. He saw commoners kneeling along the road with their heads bowed to the ground as they passed by. His eyelids felt heavy and the warmth emitting from his back was oddly comforting. He gradually rested his entire weight against the warm heat and fell asleep.

Khai with one arm tightly wrapped around his Prince's waist, had his heart almost beating out of his chest. The prince had fallen asleep on him and Khai was trying his best not to let him fall off their horse. He felt something bulbous around the prince's navel and he was immediately reminded of the body chain he saw the prince wearing the very first time he laid eyes on him. The ride back to the palace was rather torturous. Warmth stirred in his nether region as he felt his crotch hardening rapidly with every strut of his horse, rubbing against the tailbone of his Prince and he was glad that his Prince had long fallen asleep.

CHAPTER 6

1500 B.C.

Back in their palace, Khai had the sleeping Prince in his arms as he made his way to the West Wing. Servants and chambermaids trotted behind him and Khai ordered two guards to station at the entrance of the prince's chambers.

"No one else is allowed to step foot here except the prince's personal chambermaids and myself."

The guards with spears bowed their heads. "Yes, my King."

He swallowed hard when he looked down at his husband's exposed neck, his milky white skin was inviting. He laid the prince on his bed and felt his heart clench at how endearing he looked while he was asleep— the prince's lips were slightly pouting and Khai almost leaned in to place a kiss on them. But he had promised his Prince that he would not do anything that would make him uncomfortable and so he held back.

The night did not turn out as he had planned. He had wanted to surprise the young Prince with his own richly decorated private chambers and they were supposed to consummate their wedding.

The prince was still donning his wedding shoulder sash. Khai, as much as he wanted to claim the prince's chastity, he did not want to do it without his knowledge.

"Give the Prince a change of attire. I have prepared a night robe in his closet. Once you are all done, leave the chamber."

Chambermaids hurried to the prince's side. Khai quickly cleared his throat and left when he saw one of the chambermaids unloosen the robe's knot off his shoulder.

When the chambermaids were done and were just about to leave, Khai thought he saw a few of them with blushed cheeks. He was about to re-enter the prince's sleeping chamber when he heard a racket down the hallway towards the entrance of the chambers.

"You cannot enter, Your Highness."

Princess Nari glared at the two guards with spears, her hands clenched into tight fists.

"I am the Princess of Begonia, I will not obey your orders, you lowly peasants!" Nari spat on the floor between the two guards.

One of the guards lowered his head. "We do not wish to offend Your Highness. But it is the Pharaoh's orders."

Nari proceeded to enter but the two guards blocked the entrance with their spears.

"Let me through!" Nari beseeched, grabbing the two spears and forcing them apart but the two guards were too strong.

"What is the commotion about?!" Khai, having heard of the ruckus down the hallway of the prince's chamber, stomped out and was surprised to see his Princess.

"My King! They will not let me through!" Nari threw the guards a death glare.

The guards resumed their weapon's position and Khai sighed, stepping through the archway and grabbed the Princess by her arm. "The West Wing belongs to the prince," he explained with a hard stare. "It is my order that no one else is allowed through except me and the prince's personal guards and servants."

When the Princess remained silent and only fumed with rage, Khai spoke again, "Just like your East Wing chambers are only allowed for you, your personal guards, servants, and myself."

Nari realized her childish tantrum and dipped her head.

"I did not see you at the wedding procession," Khai asked, not that he minded, he just wanted the Princess not to make a scene. His Prince needed his rest.

Princess Nari seemed to soften at the mention of Khai noticing her absence earlier. "I was feeling unwell, my King."

Khai hmphed and nodded. "Shall I send up a royal physician to your chamber?" Khai might not have feelings for the Princess, but she was still his wife after all. He had promised the King of Begonia that the Princess would live in comfort and luxury in exchange for tightened forces with the East.

"It is not necessary," Nari muttered. When the Pharaoh turned to leave, she grabbed him by his arm. "Will you spend the night at my chamber, Pharaoh Khai?"

The Pharaoh turned to face her, his face void of any expressions. "I apologize, my Princess. I have to make sure our guests are well in their guest chambers. Good night."

Nari gnawed on her bottom lip, displeased at how her husband had dismissed her. The Pharaoh had yet to proclaim her as the rightful Queen of Egypt. She had to protect her position. She needed to bear the Pharaoh an heir.

Sevrin rose to an unfamiliar chamber setting. His bed was bigger— its bed frame was painted in gold, its legs carved into shapes of sphinxes.

"You're awake, my Prince?"

Sevrin jolted and pulled the eiderdown closer. He turned to see the Pharaoh leaning against the archway of his chamber, already dressed in his King's attire, arms folded across his exposed chest.

He took a peek underneath his eiderdown and was surprised to see he had donned on a silken night robe. He let a hand wander down his body and was shocked to find out that he did not have his body chain on.

He heard the Pharaoh chuckle as he entered.

"We..." Sevrin hugged his knees underneath the duvet. They were supposed to consummate their wedding last night but he didn't remember anything after the wedding feast.

Khai sauntered over to the prince. "I had the chambermaids change you out of your wedding robe." He paused to study his husband's expression.

Sevrin only looked up at the Pharaoh, confusion lining his forehead. He did not even remember kissing his husband. Clutching onto his night robe, Sevrin blushed. Had the Pharaoh, his husband, seen everything?

"I did not spend the night here if that is what you are pondering about," Khai spoke delicately as if the prince would break if he spoke any louder. "I had promised you that I will not do anything that makes you uncomfortable, didn't I?"

Sevrin watched as his husband sat beside him and his heart raced. Pharaoh Khai lifted a hand and cup a side of his cheek, his deep warm orbs bore into his.

Khai wanted to kiss his husband, the prince's lips looked plush and inviting. He tore his eyes away and stood up, clearing his throat as he calmed his erratic heart. "Come to my study chamber when you have freshened up. I have prepared a wedding gift for you."

Sevrin grabbed the eiderdowns closer to him. He had woken up this morning with a part of him that needed his attention down south. Having the Pharaoh's exposed chest and abs around him was not helping, he only found himself blushing.

"But I did not prepare any gifts for you, Pharaoh Khai…" Sevrin felt guilty, for his husband had arranged their entire wedding, put together a lavish private chamber for him but he had done nothing for the Pharaoh.

Khai's heart swelled at the thought of one day receiving a gift from his Prince. He closed the distance and tilted his husband's chin up, his thumb lightly caressing the skin beneath the bottom lip. "You are already a gift to me, my beautiful, beautiful Prince. Do not think of yourself any less."

Sevrin curled his bottom lip between his teeth. His husband's fingers were smooth and warm on his chin. A part of him wanted more than just a mere caress.

With that, Khai left his chamber, leaving him in a flustered mess. A cold bath would help soothe the ache down south, he surmised.

The Pharaoh wasn't in his study when he entered. His golden chair was empty, his table, however, a clear mess of carving tools and a half-engraved clay.

"I am sorry to have kept you waiting, my Prince."

Sevrin turned and gasped. There, standing under the archway was the Pharaoh but that was not what caught his eyes. On the Pharaoh's thickly veined forearm stood a falcon— its lower body had the silkiest black feathers, its crown was white, and it had a pair of heterochromia eyes— bright blue and red.

He was startled when the majestic bird spread its wings.

"This is for you, my beautiful Prince." Khai took cautious steps towards the prince who retreated a timid step back. "His name is Horus."

Sevrin clenched his fists at his side. The falcon looked intimidating with its blue-red eyes. When the Pharaoh gave him an assuring smile and nod, he extended a shaky hand towards the eagle. Horus cocked an eye at him before extending its neck out to sniff his hand. "Horus…" his eyes twinkled when Horus let him pet his wings.

"He is a specially trained falcon. Whenever you need to send a missive back home," Khai points to Horus' claws. "Tie it here and he will fly to Warania in just a day."

Sevrin was touched, he almost wanted to sob but he held back, his nose, however, had a tingly feeling and he hoped it hadn't turned red. "That is very sweet of you, Pharaoh Khai." Sevrin gathered his courage and reached out to his husband's free hand.

Khai's heart thumped heavily. He had not expected the shy and quiet Prince to make the first move. He tightened his hold on the prince's soft hands. "My Prince, you have not a clue how much I wanted you," Khai let his fingers interlace with his husband's, nerves under his skin sparked at how soft the prince's fingers were. "Ever since I met you, you are the only one I want to have, to keep, to protect, and to love."

Sevrin blushed. The Pharaoh's words of confession tugged on his heartstrings.

Khai let go of the prince's hand and reached up to graze his jaw instead, his thumb feeling the smooth skin of his cheek. "May I kiss you, my beautiful Prince Sevrin?"

Sevrin lightly gnawed on his bottom lip and gave a shy nod of his head.

Khai let out an exasperated breath. The prince's eyelashes bated as he leaned in, and with a tilt of his head, he pressed his lips against his husband's soft ones.

Present day

Shohan had not abandoned Pharaoh Khai Tutankhamen's tomb. A part of him tried to convince himself that what he saw and interacted were real but another part told him it was all made up in his head. He didn't know what to believe, he didn't tell anyone either. Instead, he needed a breather. So, he had convinced his junior intern, Bentley, to go on a tour to the temples of Egypt with him.

Bentley had his nose buried in a guidebook of one of the temples. "There's so many. I can't make up my mind which to visit first!" Bentley jumped excitedly beside the archaeologist.

"Well, people always start with either the nearest or the most popular," Shohan suggested with a shrug.

Bentley pointed to one section of his guidebook. "This then. How about this one?" The shorter male looked up at his senior.

"Karnak Temple?"

While his junior intern had excitedly disappeared to explore the temple on his own, the young archaeologist ventured into the courtyard. The temple's courtyard was opened to the sky, allowing the sun's rays to bathe the gravel underneath. He wondered if the ancient villagers and commoners had any understanding of what went on in the temple.

Pottery, jars, and other ritual objects were enclosed in a glass cabinet while tourists gathered around to admire the beauty left by the ancient Egyptians. Shohan joined up with the group of tourists and began reading the template.

"This jar was said to have contained oil blessed by the high priestesses for the Pharaoh's wedding procession. It was found in 1940 and was said to have been made around 1500 B.C."

Shohan nodded and proceeded to read about the other ancient objects on display.

The archaeologist, even though having studied for years about Ancient Egypt, was still highly enamoured. The structure of Karnak Temple, after thousands of years of being built, still held the power and grandeur to astound its viewers.

Ceilings were surrounded by innumerable scenes of Gods, Deities, and Pharaohs. Everywhere he looked, pictorials were always painted with the Gods. The holy temple was enormous, it consisted of a series of complex stone buildings that sprawled over hectares. Even thousands of years had not stripped the temple of its grandeur although much of the pictorials had lost their life and colour.

Shohan was once again being drawn by the engraved hieroglyphs on the walls.

"To step into the temple was to enter the realm of the Gods."

The archaeologist was never a religious person, he did not believe in life after death or reincarnation. But earlier today, he began to have his doubts.

"Rituals were essential for maintaining the cosmos."

The temple was still treated with great reverence. Priests today still conducted rituals, offering bread and wine to the shrine of Sun God Ra. He watched as a small number of priests began scattering pure white sand on the floor of the sanctuary and muttering chants he could not decipher.

"It was in the temple's sacred ground, where the sky, earth, and netherworld came together."

He heard a small sniffle and a sob and turned to see his junior intern, Bentley, one hand clasped over his mouth, his guidebook tightly gripped under his armpit as he continued to sob while looking at a display cabinet.

"Hey, you're embarrassing. What are you crying about?" Shohan playfully shoved the shorter male.

"It is so beautiful!" Bentley's words were a high-pitched whine as he cried. He rested his palm against the glass cabinet that occupied half the room and was taller than men.

Shohan looked into it. It was a golden sedan with a canopy. Its armrest had carved ornaments of Sphinxes on both sides, the chair's legs were carved and curved with serpents adorning different colours.

"I mean look! It was said that the Pharaoh had custom-made this sedan for his beloved for their wedding!" Bentley's voice cracked at the end of his sentence and he started fanning his tear-stricken eyes and cheeks.

The archaeologist rolled his eyes and chuckled.

"We can never find men like this, Dr. Shohan. It makes me wanna travel back in time and be one of the Pharaoh's beloved." Bentley sighed and rested his forehead against the glass cabinet as if that could take him closer to the past. "I wouldn't even mind being his hundredth concubine."

Shohan raised his eyebrows at his over-emotional intern and grabbed his wrist, prying him away from the display. "C'mon, people are staring. Not at the golden sedan but *you*."

They spent the next several hours touring the different temples. The last one on his intern's list was Luxor Temple. Bentley once again disappeared on his own.

Circular stone pillars with engravings created a walkway towards the entrance of the temple. The entrance had a template that gave an overview of the history of Luxor Temple.

"The Luxor Temple was the last built temple in 1500 B.C. Its building was incomplete. It was said that the Pharaoh had abandoned it when Egypt was met with war and it had remained as it was ever since."

Why had the Pharaoh abandoned it? Why was there a war? Did someone want to overthrow him and claim the throne of Egypt?

Questions surrounded his muddled head but one particular hieroglyph caught his attention. It was encapsulated in a glass cabinet, much like the others he saw in the previous temples. It was a piece of wall that had broken into pieces.

"He has eyes as bright as the morning sun. He has skin as smooth as the softest silk."

The engravings were indecipherable in the middle, having deteriorated over the centuries.

"He is, my Prince."

CHAPTER 7

1500 B.C.

Sevrin was fairly certain that Pharaoh Khai could hear his racing heart. He did not want him to pull away. With their mouths still messily interlocked, Sevrin reached a hand up and placed it on the King's exposed chest. His skin felt warm under his and he was sure he felt his husband's frantic heartbeat pounding against his chest.

Khai wanted to give his Prince all the time he needed. As much as he wanted to deflower him right here, he had to hold back his urges. He did not want to scare his Prince away.

Khai had his fair share of fooling around with his chambermaids and chamberlains. But with the Prince, he wanted to take his time, he wanted his husband to be sure that he wanted it as much as he did.

The prince's soft hand on his chest did nothing to calm down his heart. He heard a soft whimper when he grabbed the prince's hips harder than he should.

"My King, the—"

Plato stilled at his spot as he watched his King turn around with a heaving chest. He dipped his head when he saw the Waranian Prince hid shyly behind the Pharaoh.

"What is it, Plato!" Khai screeched.

Plato shrunk at the King's voice. "My King, the other Kings are starting to leave for their Kingdom. And King Sejong wishes to see his Prince one last time." He bowed.

Khai sighed heavily and turned back to his Prince who was blushing and looking down at his feet. He thought his husband looked endearing with his thick eyelashes batting against his soft cheeks. "Let us go see our guests off. And to say goodbye to your father."

For a moment, Sevrin had completely forgotten that his father had to leave. The sudden thought of him being so far away from Warania brought tears to his eyes. He gnawed on his bottom lip and brought up his arm to wipe away his tears with the back of his sleeve. He was still dressed in his Waranian royal robe, it was the only reminder he had of his home now.

"My Prince, it breaks my heart to see your tears fall," Khai whispered, cupping his husband's tear-stained cheeks as he let his thumb wipe away another falling tear. "I promise you can visit Warania when you miss your family. And you have Horus now," Khai cocked his head towards the small window shaft where the falcon stood. "You can send a missive home anytime you want."

Sevrin sniffled and nodded. The Pharaoh held out his hand and he took it. It was heart-warming to know that his husband had been nothing but accommodating. His father was right, Pharaoh Khai would never mistreat him.

"Father!"

The young Prince let go of his hand when they reached the palace foyer. The burly Waranian King opened his arms for his Prince and enveloped him in a hug.

Khai's chest tightened. He wished his father was still here. Having had wives and sons after Khai, his father hardly had time for him and his mother. Not to mention his half-siblings had all passed away at an early age due to the fact that his father was forced into multiple incestual marriages and they were unfortunately born with deformities.

Khai watched his now father-in-law give him a smirk as

he hugged the sobbing Prince. Anyone would have figured that the two had been on a lip lock just moments ago.

"You are no longer a boy, my little princeling," King Sejong chimed, chuckling as he tried to pry his son away. "You are now a man, a Pharaoh's husband. And I am very proud of you, Sevrin."

Khai walked towards the father and son. "King Sejong, you have my word. I promise to take care of Prince Sevrin for as long as I shall live."

King Sejong nodded with a firm smile. "I trust you, Pharaoh Khai."

Sevrin felt his father's strong arms prying his lanky arms off. His father cupped his tear-stricken face before leaning down to press a firm kiss on his forehead. It only made his tears flow more.

"I will leave now, my son. I wish you a happy and long-lasting marriage," King Sejong gave his son a final bone-crushing hug. "I love you." He whispered in his ear.

It pained him to leave his youngest son so far away from home. He had been there for each and every one of his son's steps and now he had to set him free. "Remember, I am just a missive away and Warania will still be your home."

Sevrin bit down on his bottom lip, almost drawing blood, as he watched his father climb into his horse carriage. He did not have the heart to watch his father leave. As the horse carriage strutted out of the palace foyer, Sevrin ran as fast as he could back to his chamber in the West Wing.

Khai's heart tore at how heartbroken his Prince was. He knew the prince needed his time to come to terms with the fact that he was now married and had to be away from Warania. With a worried mind and heavy heart, Khai continued to see off his other royalty guests alone.

His chamber guards had given him a concerned look when he dashed past them. The guards had tightened their hold on their spears thinking the young Prince was being harassed or attacked.

He threw himself over the featherbed and ducked beneath the duvet, curling himself into a fetus position. Millions of thoughts ran in his mind. What if he had not accompanied his father here in Egypt, would his father still have cancelled his wedding with Prince Soho of Saracca? If he had met the prince, would he have any feelings for him? Was his mother happy that he married a King instead and not a Prince?

He heard approaching footsteps before the corner of his bed dipped.

"Prince Sevrin…"

It was Pharaoh Khai and his voice sounded hurt.

When Sevrin didn't react, his husband sighed and spoke again in his softest voice. "If you are still upset, I can arrange a carriage for you to go home. You can come back to me when you are ready."

Sevrin softened at that. He knew the Pharaoh was understanding but he did not know he would be this accommodating. He felt childish for his earlier behaviour. He remembered his father's words before he left, that he was now a King's Prince, a husband.

He drew the duvet over him and saw pain etching on the Pharaoh's expression.

"I am not leaving you, Pharaoh Khai." He spoke in his quietest voice. "I just… I have never not had anyone around me."

Khai's heart ached. The prince was young. While Khai had lost his father when he was nine, fought and won battles, watched all his half-siblings pass on, and spent most of his childhood building an empire, the Waranian Prince, however, still held on to his innocence. Khai did not want to take that away from him.

"You'll have me," Khai scooted closer to his husband and reached a hand out to swipe away a lock of hair that was covering his eyes. "I am now your family too."

When Pharaoh Khai let his hand linger around his cheek, Sevrin found himself chasing after the warmth of his hand. His husband seemed to have noticed as he placed a palm on his rosy cheek.

Khai gazed into the prince's soft orbs and felt himself falling deeper. "I can wait for you but I cannot lose you, my Prince."

Sevrin felt his cheeks heated up. His heart was swooned by the Pharaoh's words of affection. "I am not leaving you," he let out in a breathy whisper.

Khai's lips curled up into a smile. His Prince had wanted to stay, he had wanted him. They locked eyes for a brief second before Khai leaned down and lightly grazed his husband's bottom lip with his.

He could still taste the salty taste of his Prince's tears on his lips and it tore a piece of him apart. "I will not leave you either, my beautiful."

Sevrin felt blood rush to his loins as Pharaoh Khai licked his bottom lip, a hand trailing down to his neck, thumb lightly brushing against the jut of his adam's apple. His husband's touches were gentle as if he was afraid he would break him. He did not know what to do with his hands. Sevrin always knew he liked men but he had never explored further than developing crushes on other Princes and noblemen.

Khai let out a dragged-out moan when his Prince parted his lips. He chased after his tongue and when he felt his husband's slick tongue against his own, he could not help picturing how it would feel around his cock. Carnal urges took over him when he felt his Prince laying his soft hands on his chest. Khai shoved one knee between the prince's legs but the latter closed his thighs around him. Khai soothed his palm against the young Prince's heated cheeks. "My Prince. I will not do anything that will hurt you or make you uncomfortable," Khai purred, lowering his head to graze his lips along the prince's soft jawline. "Do you trust me?"

Sevrin was laying pliant under his King. He did not know what to do but whatever the Pharaoh was doing to his body, he craved it. With a shy nod, Pharaoh Khai smiled and chased after his lips again.

Khai started to peel the silken waistband off his husband. He could feel the outlines of the prince's body chain and his cock twitched in anticipation. The young Prince's innocence only excited him more.

"So beautiful…" he heard Pharaoh Khai rasped above him when he completely stripped him of his Waranian robe. Sevrin had his thighs parted and draped over the Pharaoh's muscular ones and he felt greatly exposed and the need to close his legs but the King only placed his hands on both sides of his thigh to stop him.

Khai's cock was tenting against his silken kilt. He was glad that he was lightly dressed. With one pull of his sash, he peeled away his kilt and tossed it across the chamber. He let his hands trail gently down the prince's smooth thighs, towards his hips but avoiding the place where his husband would be craving to be touched most. His heart leaped when the prince beneath him let out a soft whimper before he bashfully looked away.

Sevrin had never seen another man's cock. His husband was big and veiny and he felt his own cock twitched against the flat planes of his stomach.

"Have you… ever touched yourself?" Khai leaned over the prince, whose cheek was blushing so red Khai thought he might burst.

Sevrin shyly shook his head, biting down on his lip. He avoided looking at the Pharaoh, he felt exposed, yet he wanted more skin-to-skin contact. Sevrin had occasionally woken up with a soiled night robe or a morning wood but he had never once attended to it. A cold morning bath always settled the problem.

Sevrin's breath got caught in his throat when the King leaned more of his weight on him, their bodies pressed together with the Pharaoh's elbows propped on both sides of his head. His husband tilted his head and molded his lips with his own, his tongue occasionally seeking his. Sevrin let out an embarrassing whine when he felt Pharaoh Khai giving an experimental rock of his hips and their cocks brushed.

Khai went at a slow pace, nuzzling against the prince's neck as he lightly dabbed the sensitive skin with his tongue. His hands traced down his chest and he found his husband's body chain. He let his fingers curl around the chains and he felt himself getting harder than he already was.

Sevrin was already a writhing mess beneath his King. He did not know what was happening to his body, other than he enjoyed it. He wanted more. Pharaoh Khai continued to nibble the sensitive skin on his neck while he felt deft fingers lightly flicking his nipple. "Mmm-my...King..." he moaned when Pharaoh Khai gave a spot of his neck a particularly hard suck. His back arched and his cock rubbed against his husband's length. Sevrin's mind was disoriented but he felt a wave of spark down his spine when his cock leaked a trail of warmth on his navel.

"Say my name, my beautiful Prince..." Khai rocked his hips once more, feeling the glide of his throbbing length against his husband's.

The prince only whimpered beneath him. Khai let his hand trail down his body chain to his hips. His husband's lips parted when he wrapped his hand around his cock.

"K-Khai...."

It threw Khai off knowing he was pleasuring his Prince. He began slowly fisting his husband and his own cock started leaking when his Prince tightened his thighs around his waist.

Sevrin fisted the silken sheets around him, revelling in the tight heat his cock felt within his husband's warm fist. He unknowingly felt himself thrusting up into the Pharaoh's fist and a moan spilled from his lips. Sevrin never experienced such immense pleasure. He held a hand over his mouth and bit the back of it when his husband swiped a thumb across his slit.

"No," Khai leaned down to pepper kisses along the young Prince's jaw. "Let me hear you."

Sevrin wanted to touch his King. He did not know how or where until Pharaoh Khai took hold of the hand that was muffling his moans and placed it on his chest. He let his fingers trace along the tattooed scriptures decorating his husband's collar bone.

Khai continued rutting his hips while one hand was busy fisting his Prince. Seeing how this was his husband's first time, Khai gradually slowed down and let go of his cock.

Sevrin felt exposed when Pharaoh Khai left the bed. He tried to calm down his breathing but it wasn't long before his bed dipped and his husband returned with a vial of oil. He watched as the King dribbled a dollop onto his fingers, warming them up.

Sevrin sucked in a deep breath when he felt the Pharaoh's oiled fingers rubbing circles around his rim of muscles. He closed his eyes shut while his hands fisted the sheets around him.

Khai knew how overwhelming it would have felt for the prince's first time. As he continued to rub the boy's entrance, he leaned over and started distracting his husband by leaving wet trails of kisses on his neck.

Sevrin was almost drawing blood from his bottom lip and he continued to gnaw on them. "Ah!" He let out a moan and tensed when he felt the Pharaoh's finger breaching his tight orifice.

"I won't hurt you, my Prince..."

Sevrin shuddered at how low and sultry the Pharaoh spoke beside the shell of his ear. He clenched down on his husband's finger, thighs almost trembling from the burning stretch.

Pharaoh Khai smashed their lips together and this time it wasn't as chaste, the King was domineering and the low grunts he was spilling only sent his head spinning. He felt his husband's finger thrusting in shallowly.

"Is this okay?" Khai paused and held up his weight off the prince. His carnal urges took hold of him for a moment and he found himself being too rough. "If it hurts, I will st—"

Sevrin nodded and this time, he craned up and chased after the Pharaoh's slicked lips. He felt his King smile into the kiss before the latter pulled out his finger and he whined when he clenched down on nothing.

Khai dribbled more oil on his fingers and slowly inserted another into the prince's clenching hole.

Sevrin arched his back, hands flailing around to find purchase until Pharaoh Khai leaned over him and he grabbed onto the King's back, nails marking his bronze skin. "Khai... I..." he whimpered, tears brimming the corner of his eyes as he felt a build-up of heat in his lower abdomen.

Khai knew the prince was close. He continued thrusting his fingers slowly, finding the pad of nerves and when the prince spilled out lewd moans and sounds, instead of thrusting his fingers in and out, Khai began prodding and dabbing his sensitive spot.

With another hand, Khai began fisting his own neglected cock as he pleasured his Prince with expert fingers.

Sevrin was a mess as he felt the King's fingers abusing that one particular spot that is making his cock ache and threatening to spill.

"Don't hold back… S-Sevrin…"

Sevrin never knew someone could moan his name in such a sinful way. With a couple more prods, Sevrin felt himself burst white all over his stomach and the Pharaoh's hand, his rim of muscles clenching around his husband's fingers with every spurt he was spilling and it threw the King off his edge. Sevrin watched as Pharaoh Khai withdrew his fingers and knelt closer to his perineum, one hand fisting his reddened cock, his neck flushed red with his head tilted back, lips parted with an inaudible moan.

Khai let a hand trace the smooth expanse of his Prince's cum-stained stomach as his back arched and he let out a guttural groan, spilling his load onto his husband's stomach and body chain. He continued to milk himself to completion with his Prince now laying spent beneath him.

He leaned down and pressed a kiss to his husband's sweaty forehead before scooting beside to lay beside him. He let his arms wrap around his Prince's waist, pulling him close so that he had the boy's back on his chest.

Sevrin felt like he had drained the day's energy. With his Pharaoh's arm around his waist and rubbing soothing circles around his pierced navel, he found himself slowly lulling to sleep with his husband's steady breathing on his nape.

"That was so beautiful, my Prince…" Khai whispered and found himself slowly drifting off to sleep.

CHAPTER 8

Present day

For the next couple of days, the young archaeologist spent his time with his junior intern at another excavation site with the rest of his team. It was not far from the tomb of Pharaoh Khai Tutankhamen. They were still in the Valley of the Kings.

He and his team were dusting off an area suspected to have buried artifacts. A seismic scan done by Dr. Layton showed a greyish area that could not be penetrated by X-rays.

Clanging of tools and dusting of sand could be heard around him.

"Dr. Jaime!"

Heads turned towards the direction of the voice.

Shohan wiped his sweaty forehead and saw his senior, Jaime, jogging towards Layton, who seemed to have discovered something in the dunes.

"You know, Dr. Jaime has been not-so-subtly checking your ass out while we were digging," Bentley said suggestively, scraping his spade against a partially uncovered engraved stonewall.

Shohan scoffed. "Jaime, Layton, and I are close colleagues. If there is something, I would have picked up."

Bentley dropped his tool and stared pointedly at the archaeologist as if he were stupid. "He was looking at your ass and licking his lips, Dr. Shohan. There is *nothing* platonic about that."

"Stop your nonsen—"

"We found something!"

Both Shohan and Bentley dropped whatever they were doing and ran towards the senior Egyptologist.

"What have we got there, Jaime?" Shohan was let through by his group of junior colleagues gathered around Jaime and Layton.

"Bones. Possibly a full skeleton." Jaime huffed with a smile lingering on his lips.

"But this is the Valley of the Kings…" Layton trailed off, arms akimbo as he stared at the bone— a partially exposed femur.

Shohan nodded, seeming to have come to the same conclusion as his colleague. "Layton is right. This is…" he scratched his nape in annoyance as he tried to form a proper sentence while his brain was firing off questions in his head. "Out in the open? No tomb? Just a skeleton?"

Jaime exhaled and his brows furrowed before he nodded. Shohan and the rest of the team stared at Jaime in expectation. Bentley, meanwhile, had wriggled his way into their circle and started prodding around the exposed femur with his tools.

"He could have been a labourer," Jaime concluded but his expression said otherwise.

"A labourer who died before, during, or after he and his other laborers maneuvered a Pharaoh's sarcophagus into the tomb…" Shohan muttered and his two senior colleagues nodded, sharing the same sentiments.

"Erm… guys?"

The three senior colleagues looked down to see Bentley, the junior intern, squatting down in the middle of them.

"I don't think he is a labourer." The intern stated as he held up something glittering. "Labourers don't wear fancy jewellery like this."

Shohan admitted that was too fancy for an ancient labourer. Heck, it was still considered fancy for someone in this modern era. It had diamonds and rubies on every chain and it glittered under the afternoon sun. "What is that, a necklace?" Shohan squinted his eyes at said jewellery. His glasses were still somewhere inside the tomb of Pharaoh Khai Tutankhamen when he ran for his life and he was not ready to go back for it even though his eyesight was failing on him. He shuddered at the thought again.

Bentley scoffed mockingly as he held the glittering accessory to his chest. "You three nerds, this?" He laid it on his chest and the chains dangled down to where his belly button would be. It had a quartz barbell at the end of it. "It's a body chain!" Bentley's eyes bulged with a playful glint and he started to imitate a belly dancer, rolling his body suggestively. "This ancient dude is kinky!"

"Bentley!" Shohan shouted and the shorter male dipped his head in embarrassment. He rolled his eyes as Jaime snatched the so-called body chain from the junior intern.

"Okay, I want a few more men to work on this. I'll call up the local research centre to see if they could set up their 3D imaging equipment." Jaime delegated and went off with the body chain.

"You know," Bentley reappeared and leaned towards the young archaeologist in a whisper, causing the latter to jump in surprise. "Maybe Jaime is kinky too."

"BENTLEY!"

The young archaeologist sat inside the man-made tent to escape from the sweltering heat of the desert. He was packing some recovered artifacts to be transported to the National Museum of Egypt while questions swarmed his mind. Who was that man? Why was he buried in the middle of the desert with no proper burial chamber or tomb? He was definitely someone of a high social status given the jewellery he wore. If he was indeed a man with status, why was he not properly and respectfully mummified like the other Pharaohs and noblemen?

After discovering the skeletal remains, Shohan could not help thinking about Pharaoh Khai Tutankhamen's tomb. The Pharaoh, his manifestation, spirit, or whatever that was, did not seem like he wanted to hurt him. The archaeologist contemplated going back to the tomb. He needed to retrieve his spectacles back. For God's sake, it was Dior! And there was no way he was going to let his expensive glasses sit inside an undiscovered tomb.

"Keep me updated with what you're working on," Shohan exited from the man-made tent and approached his junior intern. "I'm going back to that tomb and see what I can find," he lied.

Bentley looked up with sweat glistening his face and he

scrunched up his nose, groaning tiredly. "Would you be alright alone?"

"My GPS tracker is linked to the system," Shohan cocked his head towards their tent where a laptop was set up for tracking purposes. "Don't worry about me."

Finding his way back into the tomb wasn't difficult. Most of the rocks had already been moved away. With one hand holding a torch, the archaeologist hunched and staggered in until he reached the first chamber where the ceiling was high enough for him to stand up straight.

His heart was thumping in his chest and his hands were clammy. The treasures that laid strewn in this chamber stayed as they were, so he was thankful that nobody had raided the tomb while he was away.

Shohan tried to calm his nervous heart, distracting himself by reading the hieroglyphs engraved on the limestone walls.

"During his reign, Egypt became a great military power."

Just one more chamber before he reached the burial chamber where the Pharaoh's golden coffin was laid.

"The Pharaoh was as divine as the Gods."

The tomb was so eerily quiet that he could hear his own breathing. He could see a faint light flickering down the hallway to the burial chamber and his heart rate quickened. He almost felt dizzy from hyperventilation.

He took one deep breath and held it in as he walked into the chamber.

The wooden fire torches on all four walls were lit. The golden coffin stayed partly shifted open. Shohan contemplated walking over to peep into it but the thought of the Pharaoh made him shudder.

The spirit, ghost, manifestation, or whatever it was did not show himself. The young archaeologist could not tell if he was relieved or disappointed. Part of him wanted to meet him again to prove that he had not gone batshit crazy.

Standing by the archway of the burial chamber, he gathered his courage and stepped forward, his legs taking him towards the partly opened coffin.

Shohan had seen his fair share of mummies, from greatly preserved ones to those of bad shapes. However, for some reason, the thought of seeing this mummy, Pharaoh Khai Tutankhamen, the very last King of Egypt where he had spent countless sleepless nights researching on, had scared him.

He spent the next few minutes searching for his glasses and when he found them, he was more than relieved that it was not broken. He continued to study the scriptures on the walls, carefully avoiding the golden coffin with a safe distance as he made rounds in the burial chamber.

The air around him tensed. He sensed a presence behind him. Cold sweat broke out on his back. A low breathing and the sound of bare feet against gravel could be heard. He sucked in a deep breath and braced himself to turn around.

With eyes squinted shut and hands clenched into fists, he slowly turned. The silence in the chamber was so deafening that with each step he turned, the sound of gravel against his sole punctuated the air a million times louder.

His jaw was clenched tight as he mustered the courage to open his eyes.

It was the same man— the headdress, the kilt, his kohl-lined eyes, bronze skin, and gold jewelleries. Pharaoh Khai Tutankhamen.

The young archaeologist took a cautious step backwards until his spine hit the wall with a thud. The Pharaoh looked at him with the same sorrowful expression he saw the very first time a few days ago.

"My Prince, you have come back to me." The Pharaoh whispered with a faint smile tugging at the corner of his lips, who seemed relieved to see him again.

Shohan remained rooted at his spot. He held his breath when the Pharaoh closed the distance between them and reached a hand out. He braced himself to not shy away or close his eyes when the Pharaoh let his hand graze the underside of his jaw, his brown eyes bore into his and he could see the reflection of the firelight flickering in them.

"For thousands of years," the Pharaoh spoke, voice huffing out in strain. "I have searched for you across all realms."

The Pharaoh's hand was warm and smooth against his skin. It felt real. His touch was gentle, almost as if he was afraid that he would break him. The archaeologist's lips were trembling with fear when the Pharaoh placed another palm on his other cheek, thumb lightly caressing his skin. When the Pharaoh slightly tilted his head and leaned in, he could not hold back a whimper as he turned his head slightly with eyes forcefully shut.

He felt the Pharaoh pulled away and he opened his eyes to see confusion lining his brows.

"You do not have to fear me, my Prince." The Pharaoh's eyes were almost brimming with tears. "You know I will never hurt you."

Shohan inhaled shakily, finding the voice in him. "I am… n-n-not-not-not a p-prince…" he stammered timidly, pressing his back firmly against the limestone wall as if he could mold himself into it and disappear.

The Pharaoh shook his head in denial. "You are the young Prince of Warania."

Shohan gnawed on his bottom lip and saw eyes linger on them for a brief second as if he was something.

The Pharaoh let out a huff, eyes trailing back up to him. "Prince Sevrin…"

He took a cautious step to his left when the Pharaoh tried reaching a hand out to him again. He looked at the Pharaoh with trepidation, afraid that he had offended the entity that stood in front of him. "I am not… him," Shohan whimpered, head slightly dipping timidly. "My name is S-Shohan."

The Pharaoh's hand that had reached towards him, clenched around the air and he lowered it to his kilt. Shohan let his eyes trail down to where his kilt was wrapped and if he was not terrified out of his wits, he would have been ogling those taut abs and sternum.

He watched as the Pharaoh's chest rose and fell heavily with each breath he took. He tore his gaze away from him and it seemed like it took some great determination to do it. The Pharaoh had his back turned towards him and Shohan could make out the lines of muscles on his back, his bronze skin glimmered in that dimmed firelight.

"Ph-ph-pharaoh…Khai…?" The archaeologist stuttered. He did not know what he was doing. But there were questions in his head that needed answers. He gradually felt his fear dissipate the longer he spent his time in the burial chamber.

He watched the way the Pharaoh's shoulder tensed at the mention of his name. "Who is this Prince you talk about?"

Shohan slowly found confidence in his voice. His back straightened off the wall and he found himself taking a step forward towards the Pharaoh.

"Where is this Warania?" He took this chance to fire questions that had been bugging his mind for years since he started obsessing over the final reigning Pharaoh of Egypt.

The Pharaoh turned back to him with crestfallen eyes. "My Prince, do not do this to me…"

Shohan swallowed thickly, ignoring the Pharaoh, and continued, "Why do you search for this Prince?"

Tears brimmed at the corner of his kohl-lined eyes and he gazed longingly at the archaeologist as if he had hung the moon and stars. "You are my Prince. Why do you say that you are not?!" The Pharaoh grieved and a single tear rolled down his cheek.

"I am not him… Khai," he paused to study the Pharaoh's expression. He only hoped that he had not offended the Pharaoh by just calling his name. "I am Dr. Shohan, born on the 12th of April, 1992 and I am not a Prince."

The Pharaoh shook his head in denial, his taut chest heaving as he took in sharp breaths. "Please torment me no more, my Prince," his voice sounded burdened and sorrowful. "Say not of such words and come and be with me…"

Shohan knitted his brows together in confusion. "Is the Prince… a lover?"

He watched the Pharaoh's broad shoulders slumped, one

hand clenched tightly right over his heart. "You know I love you."

The archaeologist pulled his lips into a tight line as he contemplated what to ask next. "How did you die? Were you murdered? Assassinated? Or did you die on the battlefield?"

When he saw no response, he asked the final question that had bugged his mind for years. "Why do you not have an heir?"

"ENOUGH!"

Shohan raised his arms over his face in defence when the Pharaoh roared, his voice reverberating off all four walls of the limestone and the echo rang in his ears. Timidly, the archaeologist lowered his arms and opened his eyes.

"What just—" he whispered as he gazed around the dark chamber. The fire torches were diminished and his eyes were still adjusting to the pitch-black darkness. He raised his torch with a shaky hand and clicked. He shone around the chamber, the fire torches were now emitting swirls of black smoke and the air around him smelled of burnt oak, the golden coffin's lid that was partly shifted opened, now laid fully closed.

The sudden quietness was eerie and his heart was racing miles per hour. He worried his bottom lip as he walked towards the golden coffin and laid his hand upon where the Pharaoh's chest would be. "I am sorry, Khai."

His phone rang and his torch almost slipped from his hand. He swiped his screen to accept the call.

"Dr. Shohan! I have recovered the skeletal remains, come quick!"

"We've got some metacarpals here, some more femurs here," Bentley sing-songs as he unearthed more of the skeletal remains into a box. "The skull is completely intact, so the kinky ancient dude definitely did not die of a head injury."

"Would you stop referring to him as a kinky dude?" Shohan groaned, narrowing his eyes at his junior intern as he massaged his temples. He was still recovering from the earlier conversation he had with the Pharaoh, or his manifestation, whatever that was.

"Fine, fine, oh—" Bentley furrowed his brows at a particular spot. "Wait, is this…" the intern continued brushing sand in the abdominal area and another smaller set of skeletons surfaced. It looked like a fetal cartilaginous skeleton that was not fully formed throughout its entire gestation period but he could make out the small skull, spine, and limbs.

"Are you thinking what I'm thinking?" Shohan squinted at the smaller skeleton.

Bentley exhaled heavily while shaking his head. "So, the belly chain dude is not a man?"

The archaeologist frowned in deep thoughts. "It *is* a male's skeleton."

"But how in the world…" Bentley tapped his chin with his finger inquisitively. When the shorter male tried to readjust his squatting position to get a better look, he lost his balance and fell on his back. "Ouch! Hold the fuck up."

Shohan raised a brow at him, watching his intern dust off some sand about a foot away from said skeletons.

"Okay this is getting crazy, does this look like a bone to you?" Bentley held up a small piece of lumbar.

The archaeologist had both hands rubbing circles around his temples and let out a frustrated sigh. "Okay, you continue to dig up whatever that is, I'll get these… set of skeletal remains to the lab."

He hoped that his two colleagues had the local's 3D imaging equipment set up. He sent Jaime a text about the uncovered remains.

Five armed guards ushered him to a van as he carefully carried the box of remains with him. Excavation sites were known to be a target for hijack.

He closed his eyes and huddled the box of remains close to him throughout the car ride. Thoughts of the Pharaoh lingered in his mind.

He needed to go back to the tomb. He also needed answers as to who this Prince the Pharaoh kept talking about might be.

CHAPTER 9

1500 B.C

Sevrin woke to an empty bed. Sunrays spilled through the small window shafts of his chamber. Pharaoh Khai must have already been going around with his royal duties, he thought.

He got up and draped the duvet over his naked body and proceeded to his private bathing chamber where chambermaids had already drawn up a pool of hot water with rose petals.

The bath smelled faintly of rose oil. He slowly submerged himself into the hot bath and replayed the images of the Pharaoh last night. He felt himself blush. He hissed when he found a faint bruise near his waist as he lathered the scented water over his body and scrubbed the dried stain off his skin.

When he stepped out of the bath, chambermaids hurried over, each with a cloth, and began wiping him down. Sevrin sauntered back to his bedchamber and pulled out his chest of jewelleries. He clasped on a golden necklet with chains adorning with sparkles of rubies that flowed down to his navel and secured the barbell through his piercing.

Chambermaids laid out his attire for the day on his bed and Sevrin was hesitant. It was not his usual Waranian robe, it was a beige-coloured silken kilt with a red sash just like what Pharaoh Khai always wore. Nothing more.

He had been busy in the throne room with Plato. Fan-bearers stood on both sides as he tended to his daily duties as a King.

A guard dragged up an old man dressed in finery. He gave the man a kick on his shin and the latter knelt on the granite floor, trembling, with his head bowed.

"This is the man that had gone around extorting protection fees from the poor villagers," Plato mumbled to his Pharaoh seated on his golden throne.

Khai waved a cup-bearer over. "Speak," he picked up a chalice of wine from his servant and watched the man kneel in front of him, looking up with fear in his eyes.

"My-my-my King!" The old man cried, blood draining from his face.

"Protection fees? What are you exactly protecting my people from, may I ask?" Khai questioned in mockery.

"The Gods are angered by the sins of the people, my King," the accused man said with uncertainty in his voice. "The silvers collected were only exchanged as offerings for the Gods!"

"It seemed more like they were exchanged for all these fineries you are donning and living in comfort." Khai spat. "You do not play God in my land."

The man cried as he tried to come up with a rebut. "My King! Forgive me! I-I…. I will pledge my silvers for—"

"Strip him off his robe. He will serve his time as a labourer for the building of the monument for the Begonian Princess." Khai rolled his eyes and waved his hand for his guard.

As the morning passed, more men were sentenced to serve as laborers for the crimes they committed. Others were retained for public trial.

Khai was getting miffed with his morning duties in the throne room. He was aware that shortages of crops due to the drought of the Nile River had turned his people into resorting to unlawful acts.

"The Waranian Prince has arrived." A guard announced and Khai's mood was immediately lifted.

Khai took a sip of wine as his Prince sauntered into the throne room. "My Pffffff—" He choked on his wine when the Waranian Prince strode in with his glittering body chain bared for all to see. His pale skin was tainted with fainting bruises on his waist above the hem of his beige kilt and around his necklet.

Khai hurried over to his Prince, who only bulged his eye at him in confusion, and covered his body with his own. "My Prince! Did you just walk around the palace dressed like this?!" Khai spoke in a hushed voice. Khai turned his head around to watch his servants and Plato staring wide-eyed at the Waranian Prince's exotic body chain, their jaws falling slack.

"The chambermaids laid this out for me, I had nothing else to wear," Sevrin suddenly felt self-conscious with all eyes on him.

Khai tried to calm his heart and breathing as he ushered his husband out of the throne room, away from the prying eyes of other male servants and court members. "Plato!" Khai shouted back as he placed a hand on his Prince's bareback, urging him to walk faster. "Prepare a shoulder sash robe for the prince!"

"Yes, my King."

Khai dismissed his Prince's chambermaids and servants. "Change into this."

Sevrin had his arms wrapped around his exposed body. He had not felt that exposed until Pharaoh Khai pointed it out. He grabbed the shoulder robe from his husband.

"What's wrong?" Khai cupped the prince's rosy cheeks. "Do you not fancy the colour?"

Sevrin shook his head and his cheeks flushed. "I…" he muttered softly as he continued to wrap his lanky arms around his body chain. He heard the Pharaoh's chuckle and whipped his head up.

"My Prince, I have seen everything, you don't have to be shy." Khai let out a teasing chortle, his heart swelled seeing how his husband was too embarrassed to change in front of him. "Come, let me help."

Sevrin was about to protest but Pharaoh Khai's warm fingers brushed against his waist and it sent his head reeling.

Khai studied his Prince the entire time. He released the sash and pulled the kilt off his husband who bashfully looked away with his bottom lip curled between his teeth. He felt his nape heated up. It reminded him of the first time he had touched his Prince. He wrapped the silken robe around his husband's lithe waist before securing the end over his shoulder with a tight knot. Khai was pleased it hid the body chain well beneath the robe and the fine silk covered most of the prince's long legs.

Sevrin could not bring himself to look at his husband. He would be lying if he said he did not miss his husband's hands on him. He felt two fingers under his chin before Pharaoh Khai tilted his head up to face him. He keened when the Pharaoh let his thumb swipe across his bottom lip. "For my eyes only, my Prince," his husband whispered, warm breath grazing his lips.

"But I am sorry I cannot be with you right now. The court is expecting me in my study," Khai let his hand reach down to his Prince's neck, curling it behind his nape. "But I will see you this evening, my beautiful Prince," Khai smiled, pulling his husband closer, their chest touching and he wrapped his other hand behind his Prince's waist. "I am bringing Jafaar out for a hunt. Join me. We'll bring Horus too."

Sevrin beamed at the thought of leaving the palace with his Pharaoh. He stared into his husband's kohl-lined eyes. "I will be happy to, my King."

Khai could feel his Prince's body heat against his own. As much as he wanted to spend the remaining time of the day with him, he had royal duties to attend to. "I have also assigned a personal guard for you. His name is Kafre. I'll have him bring Horus to your chamber later so you can write to your family."

Sevrin leaned into his husband's warmth. "Thank you… Khai…" he tipped his toes and placed a kiss on his husband's cheek.

Khai was sure that with their chest pressed together, the Waranian Prince could feel his racing heart. His husband's advancement had surprised him, not that he minded. He was more than happy to know that the prince was comfortable around him, though he could tell his husband was still very shy.

"See you again, my Prince," Khai sighed and pressed a long kiss to the prince's forehead.

Khai needed great strength to pull himself away from his Prince. Being with Prince Sevrin was the only time Khai wished he was not a Pharaoh. He just wanted to be the prince's husband.

"Your Highness, Prince Sevrin."

Sevrin was looking out his window shaft admiring the far city when an unfamiliar voice broke him out of his reverie.

The man was tall, taller than him, and he had a black kilt around his waist that differentiated him from the usual palace guards, he also wore a black vest raiment and had a head of silky curly hair that fell to his broad shoulders. He had a scar that lined diagonally across his face just shy from his lips. Sevrin almost felt rude for staring until the man held out his arm where

Horus stood, sharp claws digging into his thick arm. "The King wanted me to bring Horus to you. If you are wondering, Horus was not the one who did this to me," the man pointed to his scarred face, chuckling, and Sevrin found himself letting out a breathy laugh.

"Come in. You must be Kafre?" Sevrin was still a little wary of his falcon. The bird's heterochromia eyes still intimidated him.

Kafre might have looked unapproachable with that stoic face and scar, but Sevrin saw him otherwise. The man was nothing but charismatic, especially when he smiled. "At your service, Your Highness." Kafre bowed.

After Kafre left Horus with him, his guard excused himself and left. Sevrin stood a safe distance away from Horus, watching the falcon with wary eyes.

Sevrin cautiously ambled towards his pet and sat on his chair where Horus stood by the edge of his study table. He rolled out a small piece of dried sheepskin and grabbed his writing tool.

When he was done, Sevrin rolled up the sheepskin missive and tied it with a silk string. His heart started racing when he tried to approach Horus.

He staggered back in shock when Horus gave his wings an experimental flap. "There, I won't hurt you." He patted the falcon's back before slowly reaching down to its claws. "I hope you will fly safely and get this to my father in Warania," Sevrin muttered while tying the silk string onto the falcon's leg just above its claws.

"Good boy," Sevrin praised when Horus did not flinch one bit. He extended his arm out and watched Horus jump on him, he winced when the falcon's sharp claws dug into his skin.

Standing by his window shaft, he eyed Horus curiously and extended his arm towards the window opening. "Now, off you go, Horus." Sevrin gave his arm a light swing and Horus spread his majestic wings and soared into the afternoon sky.

Sevrin was paced around his chamber and occasionally stared out his window. He was either looking into the far city or into the sky hoping to see Horus, but he knew his falcon would not return so soon.

He was bored out of his wits. He wanted to see the Pharaoh but he knew he was busy with his court in his study chamber. "Kafre?"

His guard appeared by the archway of his chamber. "Your Highness?"

Sevrin sent his guard a smile. "I want to go to the city."

Kafre's eyes bulged in surprise. "But the Pharaoh—"

"Pharaoh Khai doesn't have to know," Sevrin felt excitement bubbling in his chest. The only time he had seen the city was through a partially see-through sedan curtain on the day of his wedding. He wanted to experience it first-hand. "It's just a short trip. I want to see the city."

Kafre stared at the Waranian Prince in disbelief. He was never told to escort the prince out of the palace.

"Please, Kafre, I promise we will come back by evenfall," Sevrin threw his guard a pout. This worked whenever he wanted things to go his way. His father had always given in to him so long as he was reasonable with his requests.

Kafre sighed and smiled before nodding, a visit to the city would not hurt. "But first, you need a veil, Your Highness."

Sevrin beamed and skipped towards his chest of jewelleries. He still kept his face veil from his wedding.

The city of Thebes was thronging with people. Children ran along the streets, some had wooden sticks in their hands pretending to play sword, some clung to their mother's dress robe, and a few unfortunate ones were seen eyeing food stalls a couple feet away.

"We will tether the horses here," Kafre said, dismounting off his horse before helping the prince.

People were rubbernecking at the two, it's not every day someone dressed in finery was seen patronizing the streets of Thebes accompanied by a palace guard.

Merchants were quick to pounce on the opportunity by grabbing rolls of fine silk and pots of jewelleries, running up to the Waranian Prince, and striking up a price.

Kafre grabbed the hilt of his sword by his waist as he stood by the prince protectively. Pharaoh Khai had jokingly said that he would have his head if Prince Sevrin came under any harm. He had fought alongside the King in countless battles and the Pharaoh trusted him.

Sevrin gleamed when he spotted a familiar item a few vendors down. He ran towards it with his guard following close behind. "Ten candied figs, please."

"Ten?" The merchant's eyes widened and he eyed his attire before hurrying to grab ten sticks of candied figs. "That will be five coppers."

Kafre reached into his sash pouch around his kilt and passed the merchant his coppers. Kafre did not know why the Waranian Prince had purchased this amount of figs. "Does Warania have candied figs?

Sevrin nodded enthusiastically, holding a stick out to offer his guard who politely declined. "I used to always sneak out with my brother just so we could buy these," his heart clenched at the mention of his brother, he had missed him. He wondered where Horus was now and if his family had received his missive. "Every child should get the chance to savour these."

Kafre watched as the Waranian Prince approached a little boy who was grabbing onto his mother's dress robe. The boy smiled when he took the candied fig from the prince while the mother bowed and thanked him. Kafre knew then that the Waranian Prince was like no other. He had accompanied the Begonian Princess outside the palace walls when she first married the Pharaoh three years ago and she was nothing like the prince. While the Princess was snobbish and avoided people of lower social status, the prince, however, treated everyone equally.

Sevrin passed out candied figs for every child he came across, however, he held onto the remaining one.

"Are you not eating that, Your Highness?"

He heard Kafre speak and he twirled the stick between his fingers and smiled at his guard. "This is for someone else."

Kafre chuckled at the prince's innocence. Pharaoh Khai was a lucky man. "For the King, perhaps?"

Sevrin playfully narrowed his eyes at his guard and shook his head. "No, this is not for him."

He continued to walk around the street, his guard refused the approaching merchants for him. People were whispering by themselves while looking at him and his guard, they seemed to have figured out who he was.

Sevrin's heart leaped when he saw the little boy in rags, the boy who presented a flower to him during his wedding procession. He approached the boy who was sitting by the roadside with his mother selling straw-made footwear. "Hello, what is your name?" He squatted down to meet the boy's height while the mother dealt with a customer.

"My name is Ufu." The boy was shy but soon broke into a wide smile upon realizing who he was. "You are the prince!"

Sevrin chuckled as heads turned towards him. "I want to thank you for the flower you gave me, Ufu. Here," he handed the boy the last candied fig.

The mother and son thanked him with a bow. The little boy waved, suckling on the candied fig as he watched Sevrin and his guard leave.

"I see why the Pharaoh is so smitten by you, Your Highness," Kafre blocked the prince from an incoming horse pulling a wagon. "You have a big heart."

Sevrin blushed at the compliment.

Merchants on boats docked along the riverbank selling goods from lands faraway. He recognized some of the silk patterns from Saracca which his mother loved.

"I want to buy something for Pharaoh Khai," Sevrin said as they continued walking down the river bank. "But I do not know what he fancies."

"He used to love gold jewelleries," Kafre said. "Until he met you." He glanced down at the prince whose cheeks were now rosy as he gnawed on his bottom lip. Kafre huffed out a chuckle and said, "The King loved rubies and necklets, he will be very happy if you got him one."

Sevrin looked up at his guard. "Help me choose one."

The pair managed to stop at one of the boats further down the river bank.

"That will be fifty silvers," the merchant handed him a golden necklace with the brightest ruby he had ever seen.

Kafre passed the silvers to the merchant while the prince admired the ruby under the sunlight. "Your Highness, we must head back now before the King flips the palace over to look for you."

Sevrin carefully placed the ruby necklace in his sash. He hoped Pharaoh Khai would love it.

Khai had a long day with his court members hounding him with political matters. He also missed his Prince.

"Where is Prince Sevrin?" Khai hurried out from the prince's chamber to the two guards standing by the archway of the West Wing.

The guards worriedly licked their lips with their heads bowed.

"I said, where is the prince!" Khai roared and the two guards cowered, abandoning their spears and lowered to their knees, heads bowed to the floor.

"My-my… King! Prince Sevrin…. he…"

Khai grabbed one of the guards by their neck and shoved him against the wall. "Where is he!" He bellowed, his voice reverberated off the palace walls. Khai swore he would not forgive himself if his Prince came under any harm.

The guard choked and cried. "He… he… went to the city with Ka-Ka-Kafre!"

Khai released the guard who fell on the floor and broke

into a series of coughs.

"Get my horse." Khai balled his fist and clenched his jaw tight. He trusted Kafre that he would not let the prince come to any harm but Khai could not help being worried.

"Y-yes, my King."

While Khai was waiting for his servants and guards to saddle up his horse, he could not help pacing around the palace foyer.

"My King, your horse is ready," said a guard but Khai was distracted by two approaching figures over the guard's shoulder.

"My Prince?" Khai ran over to the Waranian Prince with his lower face covered by a veil.

"Pharaoh Khai," Sevrin bowed, he was not expecting to see the King by the foyer.

"And you!" Khai fisted Kafre's raiment collar but the Waranian Prince squeezed himself between both men.

"It was me who told Kafre to take me to the city," Sevrin

pleaded, although he knew the King would not hurt his guard. When Khai only glared at Kafre who stood still behind him, Sevrin continued, "he said no but I insisted. He was only obeying my orders."

"The prince could have gotten hurt." Khai's eyes remained on the guard as he released his fist. His Prince was right, he was not hurt and Kafre was his most loyal guard. However, he could not help feeling protective over the Waranian Prince who did not seem like he could wield a sword to fend for his life.

Kafre bowed. He knew better than to speak more in this situation.

Sevrin watched the way his husband's exposed chest rose and fell, his nostrils flaring as he continued to glare at his personal guard. Sevrin splayed his palm against the Pharaoh's warm taut chest and his husband's transfixed expression immediately softened. "Khai...." Sevrin threw the Pharaoh his signature move, looking up at him through his eyelashes like a kicked puppy. They had only recently gotten married but Sevrin knew the palm-on-chest move was the way to distract and calm down his Pharaoh.

Khai closed his eyes for a moment and placed his hand over where his Prince's hand was on his chest. He took in a deep breath and rearranged his emotions. "Right. I am relieved you are not harmed," Khai reached up to grab the prince's chin with his fingers and stared into his soft orbs. When his husband threw Khai a raised brow, Khai grumbled under his breath and glared at Kafre again. "Forgive me, Kafre. But not a second time without my knowledge," Khai raised a finger as a warning to both his Prince and his guard.

When his Prince broke into a smile, Khai found himself smiling too. "Now, do you still want to go on a hunt with me and Jafaar or are you tired from roaming the city already?"

Sevrin only nodded.

"Kafre, round up a few guards. I will go and get Jafaar. My Prince, shall we?"

Sevrin took his husband's hand and the Pharaoh led him back into the palace. He could not wait to present his King with the gift he bought.

CHAPTER 10

Present Day

The cool air condition in the lab was refreshing compared to the sweltering heat of the desert.

"Jaime, Layton," Shohan hugged the box close to his chest as he pushed the door open by leaning his weight against it.

"Is that the skeleton Layton saw?" Jaime hurried over to his side to help him settle the box down onto the table while Layton was setting up the 3D Imaging equipment with the local techs. Whatever tests they had to do henceforth required utmost care, skeletal bones are extremely fragile after thousands of years, especially ones that were not mummified and exposed to the harsh weather of the desert.

The young archaeologist sighed and pinned Jaime with a concerned look. "Not just one. Look," he lifted the cover and pointed to a slightly curled-up fetal skeleton positioned at the abdominal area. "What do you think of this?"

Jaime frowned, lips curled between his teeth while he stared at the box of remains. "Its cranial skull is not fully formed," the senior Egyptologist bent to have a closer look. "This could either be a prematurely born fetus or…" he trailed off in thought.

Shohan knew his senior was coming to the same conclusion as him. "An unborn child."

Jaime straightened his back to pin him with a questionable look. "But we have confirmed this is a male's skeleton," he pointed at the adult remains.

"I know what you are thinking, Jaime. I know I may sound ridiculous right now," Shohan had both palms held in front of him to convince his senior to listen to his theory. "But I want to extract both their DNAs."

Jaime folded his arms in front of his chest, hips cocked to one side as he listened to his colleague. "You're saying…"

Shohan nodded his head, eyes studying Jaime's expression for any signs that he might think that he had gone mad. "I can't be sure. I will have to run their DNA sequence."

Jaime sighed and nodded. "Okay. You do whatever you have to do. The 3D imaging equipment is more or less set up. If we can put a face to this… anyway, let me know when you have done extracting the bone marrow."

Shohan nodded and grabbed a pair of latex gloves. "Okay. Oh and, Jaime!"

Jaime turned halfway to meet his colleague who seemed troubled. "You okay, Shohan? You seemed pretty… out of sorts these few days."

The archaeologist shook his head. "I'm fine, Jaime. I just wanted to tell you that these two were not the only skeletons in that area. Bentley is currently working on another that was just right beside these. He may come in later so don't turn off the imaging equipment after this."

Jaime nodded. "Okay."

1500 B.C

Guards were saddling up their horses. They were some of the Pharaoh's most trusted and loyal guards.

"What is going down in the foyer?"

The Begonian Princess asked on the third storey veranda overlooking the foyer.

"His Majesty is going out for a hunt with Jafaar… and his Prince," said one of her chambermaids Nari had personally picked.

Nari scoffed and rolled her eyes at the guards with their horses. "That stupid cat," she mumbled and overlooked her shoulder. "I want to see Bayan in my chambers. Now."

Nari sauntered back to the East Wing with her chambermaids and guards trotting closely behind.

"This is high treason!" Bayan whispered even though they were in the privacy of the Princess's chambers.

Nari let out a peal of condescending laughter. "Oh, Bayan. I am not asking you to do it. Just tell me what I need to gather."

The sorcerer timidly looked down at his feet. He seemed to be contemplating his choices. The old man in black tunic sighed heavily before nodding his head in defeat. He could not disobey a royalty, no matter how powerful his skills might be. "A strand of hair and a worn garment or jewellery."

Nari smirked and turned to her chambermaid. "You heard the man. Make haste."

The chambermaid bowed and said, "Yes, Your Highness."

Nari watched her chambermaid scurried off. "You said this will work?"

Bayan clenched his jaw tight. He had come under the impression that the Begonian Princess wanted a blessing. "Your Highness, women sought me for my blessings. I am not certain that it works the same for others."

Nari hummed in thought. "As promised," she reached into her sash and presented the sorcerer with a bag of silvers.

The desert was fortunately not as hot now that the sun was almost setting. Sevrin kept his eager eyes on the sky, hoping that Horus would return soon. He had a bow and arrow but he saw no prey.

Jafaar had been unleashed and was sprinting across the sand dunes.

"Keep your eyes on the desert, my Prince," Khai chuckled beside him with the same bow and arrow. "Lest you want to shoot down Horus if he comes flying back to you."

Sevrin blinked several times. "What if he does not return?"

Khai found his Prince's innocence endearing. He almost wanted to abandon his weapon and make love to his husband on the sand dunes but not with his handful of guards present behind them. "He will return. Worry not." Khai reached up to curl a lock of hair behind his husband's ear.

Sevrin blushed and lowered his head. "Are you unhappy with me, my King?"

The Pharaoh gazed at him with confusion. "Why would I?"

"When Kafre and I returned from the city," Sevrin had felt guilty that Kafre had to bear the entire blame when it was him who had insisted to leave the palace. "You were angry."

Khai sighed and placed a palm on his Prince's cheek. "I was very worried when I could not find you in your chambers. Not everyone in the palace can be trusted."

Sevrin did not know what Pharaoh Khai meant but he did not question further. "I promised I will not leave you." He reassured and felt a weight lifted off his chest when his husband finally smiled.

"I know, my beautiful Prince," Khai let his fingers linger down his husband's soft cheek to his chin before tilting his head to capture his soft lips.

When they broke apart, Sevrin could hear several guards clearing their throats in embarrassment. He glanced back at the Pharaoh but the latter already had his bow and arrow held in position, one eye closed shut as he aimed before releasing the arrow. He watched the arrow disappear within the desert.

It was not long before Sevrin saw the silhouette of Jafaar, his jaws barring a dead meerkat with an arrow pierced into its sternum, as the feline proudly fetched the Pharaoh's prey back for him.

Khai reached into his sash and held out a few pieces of raw meat. Jafaar swallowed them hungrily and leaped back to the dunes once more in search of another prey.

A shrill scream came from the skies and both Sevrin and the Pharaoh craned their necks up to see a soaring falcon circling above them as if it was hunting for its prey.

"Looks like Horus wants to join in the fun."

Sevrin heard the Pharaoh say and he found himself beaming with joy when he spotted a tied missive around Horus' claws. But then his smile immediately faded when he realized that he did not know if that missive was from Warania or if Horus had lost his way and came flying back with his own.

Khai whistled into the sky and Horus immediately came flying to him and perched itself on his shoulder.

Sevrin's heart raced when he realized the missive looked different and was tied with a different coloured string.

"We should head back since it is getting dark. And then you can read what your family wrote to you." Khai knew his Prince was in low spirits since he released Horus and had been anxious for its return.

Khai chained up Jafaar to the bridle of his black warhorse. He was about to mount when he realized the Waranian Prince was standing behind him with blushed cheeks. "I want to ride with you…. Khai."

There was something about the way the prince said his name that always sent his heart fluttering in his chest. It made him feel like he was not burdened with royal duties or had the entire empire on his shoulders. He just felt like a husband. Just a husband to his Prince.

"Of course," Khai held both hands around the prince's svelte waist and hoisted him up to mount his warhorse which was taller than the other horses. "Thought you would never ask," Khai mounted behind him and wrapped a hand protectively around his husband's waist. His heart thumped crazily in his chest as he was reminded of the day of their wedding when the drunk Prince had ridden back to the palace with him while leaning all his weight on his chest.

Khai might have purposely slowed down his warhorse. He wanted the ride to last a little longer.

Present day

Shohan paced back and forth in front of the centrifuge

machine. He needed to separate the DNA from its serum before he could run more tests.

When the spinning machine finally stopped and beeped, the archaeologist carefully extracted the two Eppendorf tubes. He held it towards the lighting and watched the separated liquid in both tubes. Smiling to himself, Shohan hurried to his workbench and began the procedure to extract both DNAs.

While the system ran the test, Shohan decided that since there were still DNA samples left, he would clone them for future studies. He had a hand steadily holding a micropipette when the doors to the lab burst open.

"Fuck! You scared the shit out of me, Bentley!" Shohan cursed and abandoned his micropipette to place a palm against his chest to calm down his heart. "Do you know how long it took for me to extract their bone marrow?!"

Bentley winced. "I'm sorry! But you have to come and see this!"

The archaeologist abandoned his workbench and followed his intern.

Bentley placed his ID card against the scanner before the doors of the hallway slid open. The research facility, having contained thousands of recovered artifacts, tombs, and mummies, was highly secured. "I dug up the other remains beside the two skeletons we found."

"Please don't tell me it's another fetus."

Bentley shook his head. "It is not human. It's an animal. And a very big one." His intern sounded frustrated with his findings. "Some of its bones were missing, I suspect it had decomposed over the centuries. The imaging equipment could not pick up its reading on the animal skeleton."

Shohan frowned. "What about the adult skeleton?"

Bentley pinned him with a worried look as he tapped his card against the card reader of the Imaging Department's door. Once it beeped open, the two stepped into the room where a group of techs including Layton and Jaime was gathered.

Shohan had his heart in his mouth as all heads turned towards him. They were gathered in front of a screen.

Bentley tugged on his arm to pull him forward while a few techs made space for them.

The young archaeologist's jaw fell slack when he looked at the screen.

Bentley then said in a hushed voice beside him, "he looks like you, Dr. Shohan."

Shohan walked closer to the screen and analysed it. Bentley was right, the image, no, the *face* on the screen was an uncanny resemblance to him.

"Dr. Shohan?"

He blinked and snapped himself back to reality. Jaime was

waving a hand in front of him. "Eh?"

"I know it is rather shocking but you will not believe what Layton found," Jaime spoke slowly while eyeing the archaeologist who seemed to be still recovering from his shock.

"What is it?"

Layton turned his chair around. "This person was not an Egyptian. We compared the skull and facial features to that of the ancient Egyptians from previous findings," He presented the archaeologist with a file of previously uncovered mummies and skeletal remains. "If you compare him to these, you can definitely tell this person was not from Egypt. Therefore, he definitely was not a labourer from here either."

That was a lot of information for Shohan to take in. His mind automatically replayed the Pharaoh's words back in the burial chamber. He had called him *his prince,* the *young prince of Warania.* If what the imaging equipment picked up was accurate, does that mean that this adult skeleton could be a Prince from a land far away from Egypt? Royalties had a history of having marriages from neighbouring lands to form allies, so he would not be surprised if this skeleton, or this *Prince,* was a consort for the Pharaoh.

While questions stirred in his head, he heard Jaime speak, "What else have you gathered from their DNA sequencing?"

Shohan rubbed his face tiredly, still recovering from the shock. "Uh, that, I'm still running it," his voice came out exhausted.

Jaime nodded and gestured for him to follow. The two

reached a long table where a tech was piecing another set of bones. "This is the other skeletal remains Bentley brought in. It seemed like a feline's skeleton."

Layton came over with arms across his chest. "It's definitely not a domestic cat for sure."

Jaime quirked up a brow at Layton. "A lion? Maybe?"

The young archaeologist shook his head. "The frame is too small to be a lion or tiger." He analysed the skull and ribcage.

"What do you think?"

Shohan curled his bottom lip between his teeth as he pondered, weighing his options and striking off the least possible ones. "The skull is smaller than that of a tiger or lion. The body is more streamlined too."

Layton nodded. "A streamlined torso. An animal with speed."

Shohan took one more glance at the skeleton, coming to a conclusion. He nodded to himself. He was confident it had to be this one. "It's a cheetah."

CHAPTER 11

1500 B.C

I am so happy to know the Pharaoh has been treating you well, my son. It saddens me that I could not attend your wedding. But your father had spoken nothing but praises for the King of Egypt and that puts my mind at ease knowing he will treat you well.

Your father could not be here to receive your missive, he has been kept busy with the Sarracan King discussing allies strategies. You know how stubborn your father can get about such things.

Your brother is currently obsessed with Horus, so he said he apologizes if your new pet reaches you late.

Oh, how I missed you, Sevrin. Please come visit soon, my dear boy.

Mother.

Sevrin sniffled and gazed up at the chamber's ceilings to hold back his tears. She was still, after all, his mother, and he would be lying if he said he did not miss her. He had no idea that an accompanying trip to Egypt would be his next home for the rest of his life. If only he knew he was not going to go home, he would have spent more time with his mother and brother.

He was in Pharaoh Khai's chambers as the King requested after their hunting trip while the latter paid a visit to the Queen Mother's chambers. Jafaar on the other hand was lying in front of the chamber archway, keeping watch. His husband had laid out orders for guards not to disturb them for the rest of the night.

"Thank you, Horus." Sevrin patted the falcon's feathers and held out an open palm with seed mixes. Horus gave him a peck and it startled him. He let out a gasp as the seeds dropped and scattered across the granite floor.

He spotted Jafaar in his peripheral vision, turning to study him with his ears standing on attention. The feline must have figured him to be a clutz as he turned back to the archway and laid his head down to rest.

When Khai returned to his bed chambers, he gave Jafaar a scratch on his favourite spot behind its ears. His prince was nowhere to be seen but his heart rate quickened when he saw his husband's shoulder sash robe and body chain neatly placed on the edge of his bed.

Khai only hoped that his Prince was not done with his bath. He had imagined in his head during heated nights sharing the bathing chamber with the Waranian Prince.

"You look even more beautiful like this, my Prince."

Sevrin snapped open his eyes and jolted up. He was not expecting his Pharaoh to return so soon. He subconsciously gathered more rose petals floating on the surface of his bathwater closer to him and then felt ridiculous since they had already seen each other bare.

Khai chuckled when he saw his husband's cheeks growing red, head dipping while he played with a few rose petals with his dainty fingers.

Without another word, Khai unfastened his sash and pulled off his kilt, tossing it aside. He carefully placed his headpiece on a corner.

Sevrin knew they were going to spend the night together since Pharaoh Khai had laid out orders for guards not to disturb them for the night. Even Jafaar was keeping watch.

Khai slowly lowered himself into the hot bath opposite the prince. He exhaled and rested his sore neck on the curb, the hot water eased his tight muscles and the smell of rose relaxed his mind.

Sevrin's heart was racing as he watched Pharaoh Khai's chest rise and fall, his neck exposed as he rested his head against the curb and part of him wondered what the King smelled like.

He wanted to make the night special for his husband. He still had not had the chance to present the gift he bought for him, for the Pharaoh had taken him out for a hunting trip.

Khai inhaled a lungful of air and dipped into the water and swam towards his husband. When he resurfaced and shook his head to get water out of his ears, his Prince broke out into a series of giggles, hands acting as a shield in front of his face.

He watched his Prince reach above and plucked off a rose petal from his head.

"Did I make you wait long, my Prince?" Khai tried to set the mood by speaking in his lower register.

Sevrin felt air knocked out of his lungs watching the way Pharaoh Khai's honey-toned skin glistened with water rivulets running down his chest. He shook his head. He wanted to touch him. "I wanted to wait for you... Khai," he peeked up at the Pharaoh underneath his lashes, he was not sure if the King was fine with him calling him just by his name. "But I had to wash off the sand in my hair."

Khai felt his head spin, he loved listening to his Prince talk, his accent, his voice, was enthralling. He reached up and combed his husband's hair with his wet fingers, purposely leaving some petals of roses in between his locks. The Waranian Prince looked absolutely beautiful like this, he thought. "Do you feel better now? I suppose you do not fancy the desert as much?"

Sevrin shook his head. "It is not that. I was just anxious waiting for Horus to come back." He felt the Pharaoh curling his fingers on the side of his waist underwater and he felt his cock stirred to life. He missed feeling the euphoria Pharaoh Khai had made him feel the second night after their wedding.

"And what good news did Horus bring?"

Sevrin blushed when Pharaoh Khai's kohl-lined eyes, his warm orbs bore into his. He felt his husband brush his thumb in circles around his waist. He shuddered and subconsciously scooted closer to his King. "Good words about you, I think mother likes you."

Khai let out a thoughtful hum. "It is a pity she could not attend our wedding. I am certain my mother would be very fond of her."

"I think she will," Sevrin's voice faltered towards the end when Pharaoh Khai leaned in, their noses touching. His husband's grip on his waist tightened.

Khai tilted his head and captured the prince's warm lips. He smiled through their kiss when his husband parted his lips, granting him access. He swallowed a whimper when Khai reached up to brush a finger against his nipple.

Sevrin wanted more, he wanted to feel the same euphoria he felt. Heat pooled in his nether region and part of him wished the Pharaoh would not treat him as if he was fragile. He splayed a hand on his husband's sternum, feeling the quickened heart rate beating against his chest.

Khai was getting impatient, he had planned to take the prince in his bedchamber but it did not look like they could make it. With one hand, Khai guided and hoisted his husband to straddle him on his lap. "Oh," he exhaled and sent a playful smirk to the prince when he felt his husband's half-hard cock rest against his stomach.

Sevrin only blushed and leaned in for another lip lock. Places where Pharaoh Khai's hand touched left a burning sensation. He moaned and buried his nose in his husband's neck when he felt the latter palming the cleft of his ass cheeks.

Khai started circling the prince's rim of tight muscles, the hot bath water aided with a smooth glide. He worked his husband open with deft fingers until the prince was a moaning mess on top of him, face buried at the crook of his neck.

"I... I am ready, Khai," Sevrin whimpered, not lifting his head to see the Pharaoh for he was embarrassed. He only hoped he did not seem desperate to his husband.

Khai wasted no time before reaching down to grab the base of his own cock. He aligned it with his husband's hole, then rested both hands on the prince's waist, palms running up and down soothingly and slowly guiding him to bottom out.

Sevrin felt the initial breach of the cockhead, it burned with heated pleasure. He could hear Pharaoh Khai whispering sweet praises, warm smooth hands rubbing up and down his back, hushing him in his gentlest voice whenever he whimpered in pain.

"Slowly, my beautiful," Khai hushed when the prince was almost bottoming out.

Sevrin bit down on his lower lip, almost drawing blood. When he sat down fully on his Pharaoh, he felt an overwhelming fullness. It felt nothing like his husband's fingers.

He clenched his grip onto Pharaoh Khai's shoulders, nails digging into his bronze skin, the stretch was overwhelmingly painful. He was glad that the lower half of their bodies were submerged in bathwater that was already mixed with the most premium bath salts and oils.

Khai let his palms roam his Prince's milky skin, feeling the smooth expanse. When his husband's grip on his shoulders seemed to relax, Khai pulled out a little and thrusted back in.

"OH—" Sevrin moaned, which echoed around the walls of the bathing chamber.

"Fuck!" Khai began thrusting shallowly. The sounds his husband made only made him harder than he already was.

Sevrin's eyes were half-lidded. He rested his forehead against Pharaoh Khai as he sent him into a new bliss he had never experienced before. Every thrust seemed to hit a sweet spot that only made him want more, more, more.

"I'm—" Sevrin tried to speak but the way Pharaoh Khai was building up his speed had him choking back on his own words. "My legs are tired…"

Khai sat the boy fully seated on his lap again as they both caught their breaths. His cock twitched when he felt his husband clenched down on him. With expert hands, Khai flipped his Prince over so that the latter was now seated on the granite seat while Khai was still buried deep in him.

Sevrin reached over his head and grabbed onto the edge of the curb. When Khai started to thrust in, he could hear the echoes of both their moans and the sound of water washing up the curb, spilling onto the floor. None of them bothered as they both chased after their high.

Khai was delirious. Heat pooled in his belly when he felt the build-up of his climax. He wrapped a hand around his Prince's cock and started stroking it to his own rhythm.

"Khai! I…" Sevrin tilted his head up when he felt a warm surge down his spine, he felt the need to release but part of him wanted this to last a little longer.

Khai bent down to place kisses along the prince's exposed neck. "Don't hold back, my beautiful, don't hold back," Khai moaned as his thrusts became more erratic and uneven. The water pressure was difficult for him to thrust fast enough and he was desperate for release.

"Mmmmmnnnggg…" Sevrin whimpered, writhing beneath Pharaoh Khai when the latter kept hitting that same sweet spot. He felt his body convulsed before bursting white in the water.

The prince was spent, cheeks tinted red, pink lips parted so sinfully that it only took Khai a couple more thrusts to spill into his husband.

The two remained in the bathing chamber until they both came down from their high.

Khai then bore his Prince to his bed and they made love through the night. At one point Khai was even surprised when his husband took over the reins and rode him to completion. Khai was thankful no one came to break their moment and he managed to make his husband come three more times through the rest of the night.

The next morning, Khai heard a distant whisper-shout.

"My King!"

He squinted his eyes across the chamber and saw his royal advisor, Plato, standing by the archway to the prince's chamber, his wary eyes set on the cheetah that was baring its teeth to him.

Khai still had his arms around the sleeping Prince. He smiled down and carefully pried his hands off of his husband and grabbed his kilt across the marble floor.

"What's the urgency, Plato!" Khai hissed as he tightened the sash around his kilt. He grabbed Plato by his arms and ushered him out of the chamber. He did not want to wake his Prince.

"My King! The city is… is…" Plato worriedly licked his lips as the two made their way to the King's study chamber. "People are reporting on thefts because of the lack of food. The Nile River has not—"

"I thought the priest said a second marriage will please the cosmos?!" Khai retorted with a scoff, not that he minded marrying the prince. It was the best thing that happened in his life.

Heads bowed as Khai entered his chamber and claimed the golden throne behind his study table. Plato, priests, and other royal court members were already present.

"My King, forgive me," said a priest whom Khai recognized as the one who he sent up to the prince's guest chamber and also the one who suggested that he hold a second marriage to please the Gods. "But it seems like the Gods are not satisfied."

Khai cocked his head towards the priest and narrowed his eyes at him. "And what do you suggest? I am not making a sacrificial trip. I can't leave my Prince," Khai furrowed his eyebrows at the priest's inane remark.

Agafya, his royal astrologist, stepped forward and Khai gave him a nod of permission to speak. "My King. May I suggest having a monument built for the Waranian Prince?" Agafya looked at his King eagerly. "A temple, perhaps, may align the cosmos and please the Gods and Deities."

Khai gave Agafya a thoughtful hum. "A temple, you say?"

"But my King. If you were to build a temple for the Waranian Prince," Plato came forth with creases lining his forehead. "It would take almost a year to build. Given the drought of the Nile River, the laborers will not be efficient. Not to mention the monument for the Begonian Princess is still in the process of building, we do not have enough manpower."

Plato had a point. A sacrifice will take several moons to prepare and Khai would have to make a trip to Thebes and all the way down the Nile River to Lower Egypt. He did not want to leave his Prince's side, not when they just got married.

"Halt the building of the monument. I want all laborers to start on the development of the Temple for my Prince. Plato!"

Plato stepped forward and bowed. "Yes, my King."

Khai stood up with hands on his back as he surveyed his court. "I want you to gather the best architectures and I want to see them in my study by tomorrow."

"Yes, my King."

"You are all dismissed." Khai gave his royal court members a dismissive wave and sat back down on his golden throne. He needed a name for the temple which he would be building for his Prince.

Present day

While his team was still kept busy in the Imaging Department, Shohan excused himself back to his test lab. His DNA sequencing test should be done by now.

He analysed the report of the DNA sample from both the adult and fetal bone marrows. He compared the proteins and studied their telomeres. They matched.

"Which means…" the young archaeologist muttered to himself. He shook his head when his head automatically replayed the Pharaoh's words again.

You are the young Prince of Warania.

My Prince.

For thousands of years, I have searched for you across all realms.

He needed answers but he needed more concrete evidence

to face the entity in Khai Tutankhamen's tomb again.

"That's it!" He exclaimed and started to pack up his belongings. He texted his junior intern to watch over his DNA samples and report.

He ran across the lab and almost knocked over his colleague.

"You okay, Shohan? Why are you in such a hurry? What about the DNA—"

"Sorry, Jaime! I have to go somewhere. I'll explain later!" Shohan huffed, he wanted to go but Jaime was grabbing onto his wrist.

"To where? Want me to come along? You seem a little pale," Jaime said, he could not help being worried over the younger, ever since he returned from the unknown tomb, he had been a little off. He had consulted their intern, Bentley, but the latter had only said it was just the hot weather getting to him.

Shohan reassured his colleague with a smile. "It's fine, Dr. Jaime." He had started to think that his intern made sense, that Dr. Jaime, their Egyptologist was hitting on him. So, he would only address Jaime professionally from now on. "I need to visit the Luxor Temple."

"Oh," Jaime let go of Shohan's hand. If he was going to a tourist site, there should be nothing to worry about.

"See you, Dr. Jaime. Don't worry, I'll be fine." With that, the young archaeologist burst out through the doors with questions swarming his head. And the answers to those questions, he only hoped he would be able to find in Luxor Temple.

CHAPTER 12

Present Day

Bentley had sent him a series of texts in caps, yelling at him for not bringing him along to visit the temples. But he did not need an emotional junior crying over each display cabinet.

The temple was cooling compared to the sweltering heat outside. The young archaeologist blended in with the tourists, taking pictures of artifacts and scriptures.

He remembered coming across one engraved limestone describing the prince. He had not given it much thought but now he thought that the temple could have some hidden answers he needed before facing the entity in Khai Tutankhamen's tomb again.

Certain encased cabinets of engraved stones had no translations other than stating the estimated time period and the year it was discovered. Shohan spent some time jotting down the translations in a small notebook.

"He was loved by the people. Commoners and villagers would gather

around the prince as if he had hung the moon and stars."

It was a pity how Luxor Temple was not completed during its time. Hieroglyphs were not the most well preserved either, much of its text here and there were missing, making it difficult to piece together sentences.

"The villagers danced around the prince."

Shohan exhaled out a frustrated sigh. These did not give him any concrete information as to who this Prince was. Was this the same Prince whose remains were currently in the National Museum's Imaging Department? Or was this just another Prince in the Royal Egyptian family?

The archaeologist jumped from one display to another, most of them seemed to be words of praise for the prince.

"Children would play with the prince on the streets of Thebes. The prince taught the less fortunate how to read and count. The children looked up to the prince."

He was nearing the end of the room. Two security guards were stationed outside an old wooden door that seemed to have been installed during modern times, for ancient Egypt had only archways. He briefly saw one security officer refusing entry for a mother and her young daughter but the couple made no fuss and continued touring other parts of the temple.

"The prince captured the hearts of the people and not just his King."

Shohan stood by the engraved limestone encased by a glass cabinet. The sentence seemed incomplete and it looked like part of the stone had already been chipped off. *His King.* If the Pharaoh, the entity in the tomb, had called him his Prince, and the 3D Imaging equipment had revealed the skeletal remains to resemble him, that could explain why the Pharaoh had mistaken him for his Prince.

Shohan broke into a faint smile, his breakthrough discovery had now led him here. The adult skeletal remains they had dug up from the sand dunes was the prince these limestones were talking about. The remains were the prince whom the Pharaoh had been desperately and painfully searching for.

He stopped by the door where two securities stood guard. A sign outside the door stated no persons under the age of eighteen.

The securities let him through the room.

The young archaeologist was alone in the room, no other tourist was there. But what captured his attention was not the empty room.

Raunchy pictorials decorated the walls. He blushed at the debauchery it depicted. A Pharaoh with erected phallus and another male with shoulder sash robe with his legs parted wide for the Pharaoh. Shohan's heart rate quickened, he had not expected to walk into a room filled with engraved pictorials of pornography. The same male couple was seen on every wall with various coital positions, most of which were still practiced today. Though some of the positions confused him, even when he had cocked his head sideways to picture it, Shohan just could not imagine how one balanced like that.

The doors opened and a few adults were granted access.

It made the archaeologist blush even more, he had suddenly felt self-conscious for being alone in this room.

It made him feel better when echoes of gasps were heard. These tourists must have felt the same shock when he first stepped through those doors.

Doggy position, missionary position, the infamous sixty nine and many more lined the entire stretch of walls. Tankards and chalices of wine jugs were also depicted. Shohan could only assume that the Pharaoh and his Prince enjoyed sex and wine.

He knew the ancient Egyptians had their own practices and culture but he was shocked that the Pharaoh had chosen to document his sexual escapades. Part of the archaeologist's mind went back to his encounter with the Pharaoh, he remembered his bronze skin, his taut sternum, the black ancient scriptures tattooed along his collar bones, his abs and—

No. Shohan shook his head, he should not be letting his mind run wild with someone that had deceased thousands of years ago. Though he would not deny that the Pharaoh was kind of hot. If he had met that entity, Pharaoh or whatever he had met in the tomb, in another situation, he might even have thought that the man was into Egyptian Cosplay.

A small part of the room had engraved hieroglyphs. He decided to go closer to have a look.

"For the Prince has the purest heart, the kindest soul, and the most beautiful person I ever have the honour to love, to cherish, to treasure."

His nose was buried in his notebook, rereading through the words he translated from the hieroglyphs in Luxor Temple.

Most of his colleagues had clocked out and gone back to their hostels but here he was, mulling over the skeletons' matching DNA. The young archaeologist was muddled. If the adult skeleton, no, the prince, had a child, who was the mother? The child could either be prematurely born or....

He shook his head and sighed tiredly. The tour in Luxor Temple today only confirmed his suspicions that the prince was the Pharaoh's lover. Could the Prince have a child with another and had eloped because he had betrayed his King? Or was the child both his and the Pharaoh's? There were many questions in his head which science could not even explain. Males could not conceive and the engraved hieroglyphs on the limestone walls of

Khai Tutankhamen's tomb had stated that the Pharaoh had no heir.

The young archaeologist only needed one more piece of information to confirm his suspicions, and that piece of information required him to visit Khai Tutankhamen's tomb again.

It was already four past midnight when Shohan clocked out from the National Museum's research facility. The sky was dark, the roads were empty, save for the few headlights of vehicles on the streets. He was offered a cab to take him somewhere but he did not want to attract any attention to where he was going.

So, he set forth on foot.

By now, Shohan had the map of Khai Tutankhamen's tomb memorized by heart. He knew where the treasure chambers were, the turns and narrow stairs that led to the bottom where the burial chamber was.

He took his time. Even though he had spent hours lurking and studying the hieroglyphs on the walls and the close encounter with the Pharaoh's entity, each time he decided to venture towards the burial chamber made his heart palpitate faster, his hands clammy and cold.

"Together with the Sun God Ra, the Pharaoh shall rise over the horizon during the day and bring life to the land."

There were parts where the young archaeologist had not read, for either he was in a hurry running away from the Pharaoh's manifestation or he was just too distracted by the multiple pathways and its series of chambers.

With a torch in hand, he shone the light on the walls.

"For if the Pharaoh did not make his journey to the afterlife, the sun would not rise, the River of Nile would not flow, the soil would dry and the world would come to an end."

He could see how the Nile would affect the livelihood of the ancient Egyptians. The Nile River brought trades across seas, it helped civilization to grow, the river fertilized the soil and blessed the land with crops.

He continued down the chamber and he remembered coming across this engraved pictorial of the Pharaoh standing on his chariot pulled by his warhorse with his army of soldiers behind him. Next to it were walls of scriptures.

"His reign helped build the biggest military during its time and also the downfall of its empire."

Shohan wondered what caused the war, what exactly happened that caused his empire to befall when the people had looked up to the Pharaoh as the greatest reigning King of the Middle Empire. His last encounter with the Pharaoh had not been the most memorable one, he remembered him, Khai, being furious. He could still remember the loud roar of his voice. The thought itself made him shudder.

The strewn gold treasures were still in place. Nothing was moved and he was relieved. He decided to continue towards the burial chamber.

The air around him was still, every step he took echoed around the four walls. He shone the light around. The solid golden tomb had remained shut.

What if the Pharaoh did not want to see him? Had he offended the King? Or what if the Pharaoh had come to terms with the fact that he was not his Prince and so there was no point in returning? Or what if he was cursed for disturbing the tomb of the Pharaoh and was now waiting for the end of his time?

The young archaeologist was sure he was not cursed like the other archaeologists who unearthed previous tombs. The Pharaoh had said that he would not hurt him.

He sat his torch down and sat on the granite floor, back leaning against the engraved walls. He bent his knees with his elbows resting on them as he hung his head and closed his eyes. He had had a long day in the lab and he had travelled on foot for hours to reach here, in the Valley of the Kings, hoping to come across Khai Tutankhamen again.

Shohan did not know when he had dozed off until he felt fingers combing through his hair.

Gasping, he looked up and adjusted his spectacles. It was him again, the Pharaoh, Khai.

The room was dimly lit, it did not take him long to adjust to the firelight.

The Pharaoh, with his same pair of kohl-lined eyes, void of any emotions, bore into his. He wondered if Khai had taken his time to grieve and come to terms with the fact that he was not who he had been looking for.

"You are back."

He shuddered at how deep Pharaoh Khai's voice was. He was still sitting on the floor with the Pharaoh kneeling in front of him. A Pharaoh never knelt.

"I…" Shohan tried to find his voice. "I was hoping to find you." He studied the Pharaoh's expression; he was still looking at him with longing and it saddened the archaeologist. He could never imagine having to search and wait for the person he loved for thousands of years.

The Pharaoh reached a hand out, grabbed his wrist and stood up. Shohan allowed himself to be led up. "I feared I had scared you off."

He shook his head. "You promised you would never hurt me. I … trust you." His voice came out weak and he cringed inwardly at how uncertain he sounded even after saying that he trusted the Pharaoh.

The Pharaoh let go of him but took a step closer. Shohan remained rooted at his spot. He was surprised at how calm he was feeling. The heat radiating off from the Pharaoh's exposed skin was oddly comforting, for the desert was cold during the night and the temperature underground was even colder.

"Why do you come seeking for me again if you said that you are not my Prince?"

He saw the etching of the Pharaoh's eyebrows at the mention of the prince, it seemed like he took great strength to mention his lover.

Shohan was unsure if he should tell the Pharaoh about his team's recent discoveries, about the human and cheetah's skeletons. He did not want him to vanish out of thin air again, he knew the news would definitely enrage the King. He decided to file it away for a later time.

"I… wanted to apologize for causing you distress the last time we…" he trailed off and forcefully shut his eyes. He loathed the memory of the Pharaoh's bloodshot eyes and roaring voice before he disappeared.

A warm hand rested against his cheek and he leaned in for more of its warmth before opening his eyes.

"You do not have to. Even if you are not the Prince I was searching for," the Pharaoh sounded hurt and strained, his thumb ghosting over his cheekbone and it was comforting knowing the entity was not here to hurt him. "I am still happy to get another glimpse of you… of… him." The Pharaoh took another step closer and palmed his other cheek, letting out a shaky breath as tears collected at the corner of his kohl-lined eyes. "Oh, how long I have yearned to see you again."

Shohan had not had a lot of experiences with men. He knew he swung that way but he had never had this strong pull of attraction towards one until now. He was not sure if it was sympathy for the Pharaoh, but his heart ached for the loss of the Pharaoh's lover. Just like what his junior intern Bentley had said in Karnak Temple, that no man this day would come as close to the way ancient Egyptians courted their lovers.

They stood so close that Shohan could feel the Pharaoh's breath on his lips. It felt so real, the touch, the sound, everything. He was sure these were not made up in his mind.

When he did not speak, the Pharaoh spoke again, "I never got to hold him one last time. I never got to tell him how much I loved him and still do. I never got to tell him how sorry I was that I had caused us to be … apart." The Pharaoh's hoarse voice broke towards the end and a tear streaked down his cheek.

Shohan only stood still as he gazed into the entity's teary eyes. He thought the Pharaoh looked beautiful with the firelight dancing in the reflection of his honey brown eyes. His cheeks were warmed between the Pharaoh's palms and a part of him wanted to feel how his skin felt.

"Will you grant me a wish?"

Shohan's head was spinning when those words left the Pharaoh's lips. He only nodded.

A faint but pained smile curled up the corners of the Pharaoh's lips. "Will you let me hold you as if you were my Prince?"

Another tear rolled down the Pharaoh's cheek which trickled down his sleek jaw to his chin.

Shohan was choking back a sob. For some reason, he felt the pain the Pharaoh was feeling. "Yes."

The Pharaoh let go of his face and wrapped his strong veiny arms around his shoulder and waist. He had a side of his face squashed onto the Pharaoh's exposed chest. Shohan heard no heartbeat but he could hear the staggered breaths Khai was letting out, and with each sob, the arms around him tightened.

"My Prince... my Prince ... my beautiful, beautiful Prince..."

Shohan could feel the agony in the Pharaoh's cries, his chest heaving against his face. He could not hold back his emotions as Shohan let a tear fall.

"I love you, my Prince. Why did you go... why did you leave..."

Shohan was never good at comforting others. Nevertheless, he curled his arms around the Pharaoh's waist and held him tight. It only sent Khai more anguish.

"It was my fault, if I had not left your side... my Prince, I am sorry, my love."

The Pharaoh's words of grievances tore him apart. It felt like Khai Tutankhamen was treating him as the closure he needed, the final words of love, apology, and goodbye he did not get to say to his Prince when he was alive when he last saw him.

He felt the Pharaoh rocking him side to side, one hand cupping the back of his head, it was as if the Pharaoh was terrified of letting him go, afraid that he would disappear.

Shohan let himself continue to be embraced by the Pharaoh until the latter's breaths had calmed down. The Pharaoh then loosened his grip around him and broke away, one hand curled over his nape before he tilted his head and smashed their lips together.

Shohan's eyes bulged when warm lips captured his. He had his hands clenched into fists by his side, unsure where to place them. The Pharaoh's kiss was hungry and desperate as he continued to claim his mouth, tongue ghosting between his lips, seeking entrance.

He was about to part his lips to take a breath but the Pharaoh only held him closer, tighter as he deepened his kiss, tongue tracing his inner lip before nibbling on his bottom one and Shohan let out an embarrassing moan. He had never been so passionately kissed like this before. He could feel the Pharaoh inhaling deeply through the kiss.

Shohan's mind went to places he shouldn't. He let his hand rest against the Pharaoh's warm chest, feeling the abdominal muscles taut with each of his touches. When the Pharaoh held him tighter, he recalled the engraved pictorials on the walls of Luxor Temple, and a warm heat pooled in his lower region. He reached up and carded his fingers through the Pharaoh's hair, the latter's headpiece fell with a loud echoing thud but none bothered to break apart.

His head was spinning by the time Pharaoh Khai slowed down, planting chaste pecks on his lips. The archaeologist's knees went weak but the Pharaoh's strong arms held him up. "My Prince... my Prince..." he heard him say as the Pharaoh rubbed soothing circles on his back.

When they pulled apart with their lips throbbing red and slicked with spit, the Pharaoh leaned in again and planted a long soft kiss on his forehead.

Shohan was swooned. He was a hopeless romantic and the Pharaoh was everything he had read in storybooks. He was like a Prince Charming he wanted to meet as a child.

He kept his head low, watching the Pharaoh's heaving chest, his ruby necklace sparkled in the firelight. Two fingers tilted the archaeologist's chin up so that he was facing the entity in the eyes.

"Will I see you again?"

Shohan's breath was caught in his throat. After the lip-lock they had, he could not find his voice. He only nodded.

Warmth spread in his chest when the Pharaoh smiled, though with a tinge of regret and longing.

"Can I... call you my Prince?"

He let out a breath he did not know he was holding. Pharaoh Khai's hoarse voice was even sexier after their make-out session. He knew the Pharaoh needed his closure and he did not mind being used as a vessel for said Prince.

"Y-yes…"

The entity smiled again. "Can I hear you call me your King one last time?"

Shohan did not know what the Pharaoh meant by *'one last time'* but he hoped the latter did not mean what he had said.

"Yes… my King."

He was light-headed and the burial chamber was spinning. He did not know how long he had spent down here. The last thing he saw was the Pharaoh's smile, the warmth of the entity's hand on his cheek before his vision tunnelled and he hit the cold hard floor.

CHAPTER 13

1500 B.C

Khai had been kept busy in his study. Plato had gathered the city's best architectures and they had been presenting ideas to him since morning.

He heard heavy approaching footsteps and looked up to see his most trusted guard entering his study chamber.

"My King," Kafre bowed and rose straight. "The Waranian Prince wishes to go to Thebes."

Khai contemplated for a while. He did not like the idea of having his Prince away from him.

"I can round up a few more guards if you are worried," Kafre spoke again when Khai kept mum.

Khai shook his head. He trusted Kafre, who had been in countless battles with him and had kept him safe all those times. "Do not wander far from Thebes and be back before nightfall."

Kafre bowed once more. "Yes, my King."

Khai reluctantly watched his Prince's personal guard leave his study chamber. He might personally head down to Thebes to surprise his Prince later when he was done with his duties.

"How soon can we have the temple ready?" Khai asked, forcing himself to focus on his work.

A young architect presented his calculations while others worked on the design and materials needed. "If we start tomorrow, with the current laborers on hand, we should be done within six moons, if the weather conditions allow."

"Proceed with the construction of the temple tomorrow morning. I shall appoint you to oversee the process." Khai said.

Plato then came up to him with worry lining his brows. "But my King, six moons, that is a long time. The soil is cracking, not a single grass has grown since the drought. I fear the people might resort to unlawful acts to feed their stomachs."

His Royal advisor had a point, he could not just sit and wait for the temple to be built. He needed to do something.

"May I suggest something, my King?"

Khai looked up to see the priest stepping up. He gave him an approving nod to continue.

"While the temple is in its preparation to be built, may I suggest for the high priestesses to also prepare the things required, should the need for a sacrificial trip arise in the near future?"

Khai exchanged a look with Plato. Preparation for a sacrificial trip down the Nile River all the way to the lower Egypt of Aswan required sufficient stocks. They needed time to gather.

Khai nodded. "You shall oversee the preparations with the high priestesses of Karnak Temple."

With that, the priest left and Khai slouched on his golden throne.

"My King."

Khai let out a sigh and glanced up to see a palace guard from the north wing. The guard then said, "The Queen Mother wishes to see your Majesty in her quarters."

He rubbed his palms tiredly on his face. He looked to Plato who gave him an understanding nod.

He left his study chamber with the palace guard trotting behind him as he made his way to his mother's chambers.

"You wished to see me, mother?" Khai stood by his mother's bedchamber archway. He did not exactly enjoy spending time with her, for she was always hounding him with marriages and pestering him to give her a grandchild.

The Queen Mother was having an afternoon tea snack. "Son! I have not seen you since your wedding."

Khai rolled his eyes and joined his mother by the table. "You made me a King when I was nine. I have been busy since then," he retorted.

His mother chuckled and pushed a golden tray of sweets towards him. "I had to groom you even though I had the power to rule. You are going to be the future King of Egypt one way or another."

When Khai did not speak, his mother pressed on.

"I heard that you are building a monument for Prince Sevrin?"

Khai's chest warmed at the mention of his Prince. "Yes, mother. Agafya suggested a new monument will align the cosmos."

"Ah, the Nile," his mother sighed. "I wonder what your father would have done if he was still alive today."

Khai scoffed and shook his head. "Father would be bedding the many chambermaids around the palace."

"Khai. Do not speak of your father like this," his mother reprimanded.

"Fath—"

Before Khai could speak, he was interrupted by the presence of the Begonian Princess.

"Oh, Nari, darling!" His mother beamed and stood up to receive the Princess who was bearing a tray of golden goblet.

His wife smiled and bowed to him. "Pharaoh Khai."

Khai bit the inside of his cheeks at how Nari's voice changed around him. It irked him.

"Mother," Khai turned his attention back to his mother after giving his wife a curt nod to acknowledge her presence. "I thought I had ordered the guards that your north wing was only accessible to you, your chambermaids and guards?"

"Oh, Khai. Do not be so harsh on Nari," his mother turned and smiled at his wife and also reached across the table to hold Nari's hand. He saw his mother giving Nari's hand a light squeeze. "Nari only has good intentions," his mother said before taking the goblet and sipping its contents. "My health has not been the best and Nari has sourced someone outside the palace who brews tea that treats all ailments."

Khai eyed his wife suspiciously before looking at the goblet. "I did not know you were unwell, mother."

His mother only let out a small giggle before reaching up to graze her smooth hand on his cheek. "Of course, my dear son, you have been so busy with your duties and your new Prince."

"Speaking of which," Nari interrupted. "My chambermaids had seen the prince leaving the palace with his guard. Does he visit the city often?"

"Why, do you wish to visit the city too, *my Princess?*" Khai said bitterly with sarcasm. He knew his wife did not like the desert heat and preferred her luxurious chambers. Khai had given his wife the biggest wing of the palace when they got married three years ago.

Nari threw him a disapproving look. "Why would I mingle with the peasants?" She spat with disgust.

"Now how will you two bear me a grandchild if you both are always at each other's necks?" His mother placed her now-empty goblet on the table.

Khai thought he saw his wife smile at his mother even though they were being reprimanded.

"I told you, mother, I have no intention of having her carry my child." Khai had his hands clenched into fists under the table.

His mother glanced worriedly at the Princess who did not

seem the least bit offended by his remark. "Khai, do not speak of Nari in this tone."

His wife only scooted closer to his mother which made his skin crawl. He had never seen the Princess being this close with his mother. He always thought the Princess kept to herself.

"It is alright, mother."

He heard Nari speak before he could come up with another rebut.

"I am in no hurry to have a child either, mother."

Khai was confused. He remembered Nari trying her luck in asking him to spend the night with her in her chambers. He wondered what changed her mind.

"I am not getting any younger, it is time you provide an heir," his mother smiled adoringly at the Princess before patting her rosy cheek.

Khai could not stomach the scene in front of him any longer. He stood up to leave.

"Where are you going, son?"

"Jafaar's dungeon." Khai left without sparing his mother and wife another glance.

After spending some time training and letting Jafaar have some playtime, he led his cheetah to his chambers and commanded him to stay guard. After which, he rounded up a few royal guards and saddled his warhorse. He wanted to surprise his Prince in the city. He wondered why the prince loved Thebes so much.

Thebes was just like how Khai last saw when he and his Prince passed by on their way to Karnak Temple for their wedding. Throngs of people filled the streets; the desert heat did not deter merchants from setting up their booths under the scorching sun.

Khai was donned in a palace guard's outfit, for he did not want attention on him. He led his warhorse upfront while his guards stayed close behind.

A cacophony of children's laughter caught his attention. He dismounted and a guard fetched his horse's reins to tether them.

Children were dancing around a taller figure, their smiles bright and their laughter brought life to the dull city. It did not take long for Khai to figure out who the tall figure was. His skin was the fairest amongst them all and even though he had a veil covering his lower face, Khai could still recognize those crescent moon eyes when he smiled.

Khai approached them and when the children spotted him and his group of guards, they cowered behind the prince.

Sevrin's heart thumped in his chest. He had not expected a group of palace guards in Thebes. He held out a protective hand in front of the children. He looked towards Kafre who was holding back his laughter. It was then that he saw the guard in the centre whose stance did not look like a guard at all. He stood like a King; chin held up high with both his hands locked behind him. He huffed out a sigh when the guard came closer and he could see his kohl-lined eyes.

"Children, fear not." Sevrin ignored his husband and squatted down to meet the children's height.

"Are they here to catch us? We promise not to play in the streets again." The boy in rags, Ufu, looked up to the group of guards and back at him, his tiny hand fisting his shoulder robe.

Sevrin chuckled at the child's innocence. "No, they are not. The guards are here to take me back to the palace."

The children wailed and hugged his legs, some had started crying. "Go back to your mothers now, children. I will see all of you soon." Sevrin patted some of the crying children's heads before they left hurriedly. The guards must have intimidated them.

Khai saw how the Waranian Prince's shoulder robe was

dirtied with mud at its hem, but even the dirt on his silken robe did not take away his beauty. He gave his husband a playful bow, dedicated to his role as a guard, and smirked. "His Majesty wishes to see you back in the palace, my Prince."

Sevrin giggled at how his husband was trying so hard to pretend to be a guard when the way he spoke and behaved was nothing but a King. Commoners paid them no mind as Sevrin let himself be escorted with Kafre stifling his laughter behind them.

When they reached their horses, Sevrin spotted the Pharaoh's warhorse tethered among the other guard's horses. Its black mane was silky and shiny compared to the others, it was also taller and mightier. It gave a whiny neigh when Khai approached him.

"I never got to ask what his name is?" Sevrin enquired as he felt Pharaoh Khai's strong hands on both his waist, hoisting him up to mount the warhorse. He heard a low grunt when Khai mounted behind him and arousal pooled in him.

"Zohar," Khai said and reached forward to grab the reins while his other curled around his husband's waist. "It means fearless spirit."

Sevrin had always loved horses. He remembered going horse riding with his brother back in Warania when they were little. "Can I control his reins?" He asked when Pharaoh Khai took the lead and the horse strutted towards the direction of the palace.

Khai handed over the reins and curled his free arm around his Prince's waist. He let his thumbs rub against his husband's abdomen, feeling the barbell twist in his navel. He felt his cock stirred when he curled his finger around his body chain through his robe. "You are testing me, my Prince."

Sevrin could feel Pharaoh Khai's gradually hardening cock prodding against his tailbone with each of the horse's strut. He daringly pushed his hips back. The grip around his waist tightened and he heard a guttural groan at the shell of his ear.

Khai breathed down his husband's nape and planted a kiss there. "His Majesty will be displeased to hear of such acts with a palace guard," he teased and felt the prince's abdominal muscles convulsing when the latter tried to stifle his laughter.

Sevrin turned his head halfway around to meet Pharaoh Khai's kohl-lined eyes boring into his. His heart fluttered when the Pharaoh tilted his head and lifted his face veil to capture his lips. When they broke apart, Sevrin let out a contented sigh and leaned his weight against his husband's chest. "I still preferred your Pharaoh's attire, my King."

Khai chuckled and took over his horse's reins. He felt his Prince's hand resting over his own which was still curled protectively over his waist. "Do I not look good in this?" Khai pretended to be offended which only made his Prince smile and oh, he loved the way his eyes turned into crescents whenever he did.

Sevrin's cheeks grew hot but he wanted to rile up his husband. "But your Pharaoh attire showed more skin." He bashfully turned back to the front.

Khai did not know what he had turned his Prince into. He never knew his husband could talk like that and he loved that immensely. He thought that maybe after deflowering his husband had sexually awakened him. "Oh, what have I done to you…" Khai groaned, he had initially wanted the ride to last a little longer. They rode towards the palace faster than he had originally planned. He could not wait to have his Prince all to himself.

Back in his chambers, Jafaar got a little too excited seeing his master's return and pranced towards the archway, only to pounce on the Waranian Prince.

"Nngh!" Sevrin whimpered as he hit the hard granite floor.

"Jafaar! Back!" He heard Khai's raspy roar.

Khai scooped his husband up from the floor and walked over to his bed. He laid the prince down and roamed his eyes over the latter's body. The Waranian Prince had his eyebrows pinched together as he cupped a hand at the juncture of his elbows.

"Let me see."

Sevrin let the Pharaoh pry his hand off.

Khai sat himself at the edge of his bed. He let out a relieved sigh when he saw that it was just a scratch that had pinked and swelled.

"It is not his fault… Khai," Sevrin said when he saw Khai glared at his pet cheetah. He placed a hand on his Pharaoh and sat up. "I was just a little shocked."

Khai reached over and let his hand caress the softness of the prince's cheek. "It still pains me that you are hurt."

Sevrin felt soft fur on his thigh and saw that Jafaar had his chin resting on him. The cheetah gave his injured arm a lick and purred. He reached out and scratched the back of its ear. "See? Jafaar said he is sorry."

Khai exhaled out a breath, leaned closer, and pressed a soft kiss on the prince's forehead. "You have the kindest and purest heart, what did I ever do to deserve you?"

Sevrin blushed and dipped his head. "I have something for you… Khai," he reached into his sash and curled his fingers around the ruby necklace. He pulled it out and presented it to his King. "I got this from the river market in Thebes the first time I went. It is from Valharia and the merchant said that this ruby was blessed by their high priest and that it will protect its wearer from all evils."

Khai had his heart in his mouth. His nose tingled and he felt tears collecting at the corner of his eyes. His Prince had gifted him a present and he was touched by the gesture. Khai needed no extravagant golds or treasures anymore since the day he laid eyes on the Waranian Prince, but to receive a gift well thought of by his lover was the most heart-warming thing he had ever experienced. Just when he thought he could not love his husband much more than he already did, Khai felt himself falling for Prince Sevrin all over again.

He let the prince fasten the ruby necklace on him. It was the brightest ruby he had ever seen. Khai tilted his husband's chin up and molded his lips against his.

Sevrin fisted his husband's palace guard's uniform while the latter undid the knot of his shoulder sash robe. Both men did not care if mud caked their feet or if sand were tangled in their hair. They eventually managed to get each other out of their clothing articles.

Their arms were messily tangled as both men were heated and desperate to map out every inch of each other's skin.

His Prince had his legs parted and curled around his waist as Khai let the pad of his tongue dab against his sensitive neck. The way Prince Sevrin had his back arched when Khai hit a sensitive spot near the shell of his ear had him humping the prince dry. Khai thrust his hips, feeling the glide of his cock against his husband's own throbbing one.

Khai sighed as he pushed himself up and away from his Prince. As much as he wanted to take his husband, he did not want to hurt him. He remembered storing a vial of myrrh oil somewhere.

He could hear the Waranian Prince's soft whimpers as he searched through his chamber. When he turned back to his Prince, holding the vial of myrrh oil, his jaw fell slack.

His Prince had his knees bent, legs so obscenely parted with his balls hanging heavy between his fair thighs. Khai watched his husband taking his own cock in his hand and stroking it, his balls bounced each time the latter hit the base of his cock and Khai felt his own cock twitch.

Sevrin had his eyes closed, he did not like his Pharaoh's absence after riling him up like this. He stroked his own cock, paying attention to its reddened tip before he felt the bed between his legs dent and warmth enveloped him.

It did not take long for Khai to open his Prince up. With three fingers up his husband's clenching hole, Khai stroked his Prince's leaking cock before taking the tip into his mouth.

"Nnnnggg!" Sevrin bit down on his bottom lip and reached down to card his fingers through the Pharaoh's coarse hair. The feeling was overwhelming, with Pharaoh Khai prodding his sweet spot and his cock in his warm wet mouth, Sevrin was desperately holding back from spilling. "Khai… Khai… mmph…" he moaned so loud and he was glad that they were the only ones in the bed chambers.

Khai hollowed his cheeks and took his Prince deeper and continued dabbing his sweet spot. He released his cock with a pop and engulfed one of the prince's balls in his mouth, tongue dabbing against its sensitive skin before nosing his perineum which was slightly bulging and he knew his Prince was full and nearing his climax. With a couple more prods, he watched his Prince parted his lips and let out a throaty moan as he spilled white all over his stomach. Khai could feel himself leaking when he felt the prince clenched down on his fingers with every spurt, balls drawn high and tight to the base of his cock as he spilled himself empty.

Sevrin's throat was parched by the time he came down from his high. He opened his eyes to see Pharaoh Khai's veiny cock still erected red and leaking.

"So beautiful, my love," Khai scooted up to lie next to his spent Prince. He propped himself up by his elbow as he leaned down to kiss his husband while his other hand played with the prince's come on his stomach, feeling the glide against his smooth skin.

Sevrin revelled in the warmth of Pharaoh Khai's hand on his come-stained stomach as the latter deepened their kiss.

"Hmmmm…" Khai moaned into the prince's mouth when he parted for him and their tongues curled against each other. He let his come-stained hand trail back down to his husband's cock, giving him an experimental stroke.

"Ah…" Sevrin moaned in oversensitivity but it did not take long for him to fill out once again.

Using his Prince's come as lubrication, Khai reached further down and slid in three fingers, feeling the warmth tight hole.

"Take me, my King..." Sevrin rolled his eyes back, feeling the gradual build-up of arousal again. "Please... Khai..."

Khai smirked as he gave his Prince a final suck on his lower lip and watched the way the plush reddened lip bounced back when he released it with a slick pop.

Kneeling between his fair thighs, he aligned his cock with the prince's hole and slid in. "Mmmph, so tight, my Prince..." he moaned as he bottomed out, balls snugged against his husband.

His bedchamber was soon filled with the sound of bed creaking and screeching against the granite floors, of balls slapping against skin, light-headed and the beautiful lewd noises spilling out from his Prince. When he pulled out, he could see his Prince's own come spilling out from his hole when Khai had used it as a lubricant. The sight sent his head spinning.

Khai then flipped his Prince to lie on his stomach as he rammed into him, hands gripping tightly onto the prince's soft ass cheeks. It sent Khai closer to his edge watching his husband's reddened ass bounce with every thrusts.

Sevrin was soon spilling indecipherable noises into the pillow as the Pharaoh's cock stretched him wide and continuously hit his sweet spot. "Khai!" He whined, the drag of his cock against the silken sheets with each of Pharaoh Khai's thrusts was sending him over the edge. "I am... I need to—"

"Come. Come for me again, my Prince…" Khai let out a chesty grunt as he gave his Prince a particularly hard thrust.

"Nnngh!" Sevrin felt his vision tunnelled white as he spurted. "Mmggh!" He moaned as he spurted again, his toes curling as he continued to empty himself onto the sheets. He heard Pharaoh Khai let out the dirtiest moan before he felt his husband's warm come leaking down his thighs. He clenched down on his husband as he milked him empty.

Khai, with his knees and elbow supporting most of his weight, laid on top of his Prince as he left chaste kisses along his husband's shoulder.

Sevrin winced when Pharaoh Khai palmed his ass cheeks.

"Did I hurt you, my Prince?"

He heard his husband's voice dipped an octave deeper and that itself almost made him hard again if it wasn't the fact that Pharaoh Khai had made him come twice.

"No, my King…" Sevrin sighed and smiled before turning to bury his face in Pharaoh Khai's warm chest even though he was sweaty. He did not mind. He felt safe in his King's arms.

Khai smiled down at his sleeping Prince in his arms, one hand rubbing soothing circles on his waist, holding him tight, while his other carded through the prince's soft locks as he slowly lulled his lover to sleep.

CHAPTER 14

Present Day

He groaned as he tried to sit up. His head was pounding at one side and he felt light-headed. The burial chamber's firelights were almost diminishing, one of the wooden staves was already emitting a swirl of dark smoke. He shook his head as he slowly stood up, feeling his blood rushing back to his head.

Looking around the chamber, he slowly recalled the events that happened. He held up a finger to his lips. He remembered having the Pharaoh's lips on his. Something on his hand tickled his chin while he was dabbing his own soft lips. The young archaeologist looked down to see two strands of hair.

They were not his.

While his hair was soft and thin, the strands on his fingers were coarse, thick, and shorter than his own. He blushed as he recalled when the Pharaoh deepened their kiss and he had probably fisted his fingers on the entity's hair. His heart skipped a beat. This was the last bit of specimen he needed to confirm his theory about the skeletons they uncovered. Shohan quickly pocketed the strands of hair and hurried out of the chamber.

The sun was already out by the time he climbed up from the ladder. He looked at his wristwatch. It was already ten in the morning. Shohan remembered leaving the research facility at four in the morning and had travelled on foot for a couple of hours here in the Valley of the Kings.

The tunnel shafts and chambers being more than twenty meters underground made it impossible for one to stay in the tomb for more than a few hours, for carbon dioxide was denser. He figured he must have passed out from the lack of oxygen.

It did not take long for a local to spot the lone wandering archaeologist. He offered him a price for a ride. Having insufficient sleep coupled with the early morning's events, Shohan shrugged and followed the cabby and gave him directions to his hostel.

As much as he was excited to head back to the research facility to extract the hair's DNA, Shohan knew he needed to catch up on his sleep.

He spotted his teammates in the lobby of their hostel having breakfast. Jaime was the first to run up to him and gave him a quick scan worriedly.

"Bentley said you did not return last night," Dr. Jaime said. "We almost went out looking for you. Are you alright? You don't look so well."

Shohan tried to force out a smile to reassure his colleague. "I am okay. I was at the lab all night," he lied. "I think I'll have to rest up for the day."

Layton was the next to come up to him after finishing his breakfast. "Told you he would be fine," Layton nudged the side of Jaime's arm playfully. "He was so worried he almost made the entire team go out on a search party."

Shohan stifled a chuckle. "I'm fine. But I'll have to leave my intern with you guys today," he yawned.

Layton looked both concerned and offended. "You mean Bentley? Bro, he was hugging a dug-up vase yesterday and started crying."

That did not surprise the archaeologist after visiting Karnak Temple with Bentley. "Don't be too harsh on the kid, Layton. He can be a tad emotional."

Layton smacked his lips and glared at Jaime. "I'm leaving that kid with you, Jaime. Got to head back to the lab now. Bye."

Shohan laughed and excused himself back to his room. He carefully placed the strands of hairs into a ziplock bag, tugging it away in his nightstand before hitting the bed. He let his mind replay the encounter with the Pharaoh's entity as he slowly drifted off to sleep.

After catching a few winks, he hurried back to the research facility. Shohan made a beeline to the lab where he had kept the cloned DNA samples of the skeletons. He took out a strand of hair from the ziplock bag with a pincer and proceeded to extract its DNA.

His phone buzzed while the machine ran its contents.

It was from Jaime. "If you're here, come to the Imaging Department."

He pocketed his phone and made his way there, scanning his staff ID card on the reader.

"Dr. Jaime?" The doors slid open and he found Jaime hunching over the long table where all three skeletons were laid out according to its anatomy.

"What do you think of this?" Jaime held up a piece of vertebrae from the adult skeleton.

Shohan took it with his gloved hand and examined the grey bone under the light. "It's the eleventh vertebrae."

Jaime nodded, expectant eyes on the archaeologist. "The

thoracic."

He twirled the bone around, deft finger prodding against a slight dent or possible hairline fracture. He looked at his colleague who had an eyebrow quirked up at him. Jaime must have come to the same conclusion as him. "It seemed something had punctured it."

"A hairline fracture. I'm guessing something was pierced through his back, look," Jaime wriggled two fingers at him to follow. "His sixth left rib."

He took the rib bone from him and examined it. It had a similar fracture but worse, part of the rib was already chipped off. His brows pinched together as he held both bones and looked at his colleague. "Pierced through his back and out through his chest?'

Jaime cocked his head to one side and shrugged. "It is my guess. I had sent your intern back to its location to see if he could find anything else."

Shohan exhaled out a shaky breath as he placed both bones on the long table and sat down.

"Something seems to be troubling you."

"Huh?" The archaeologist snapped his head up to meet Jaime's worried gaze.

Jaime pulled a chair over and sat opposite him. "I noticed you have been going to the unknown tomb often but you have not returned with anything. Bentley also said you have been rather quiet lately."

He rubbed his eyes tiredly. "I... I was—"

"It is okay, Shohan. I know you have been wanting to find the last King of Egypt and our excavation time is running short." Jaime reassured, reaching over and cupping his hand over his own. "If the university manages to outsource more funds to fund our research, we will come back again."

Shohan only nodded. He did not want others to disturb Khai Tutankhamen's tomb, not when he had not pieced together the puzzles. If his team had found out he had uncovered the last King's tomb, they would start removing the golds, the treasures, and they might also take Khai's solid golden coffin back to the research facility. He needed to see Khai again. He could not risk his team finding out now. He needed more time.

The doors burst open at that time and both Jaime and Shohan gasped. The lab's security siren rang. Men with masks over their heads infiltrate their lab with their rifle guns pointed at them. Jaime then had his arm held over him protectively, pushing him to stay behind him.

The men were yelling in a language unknown to them. Hijackers. Tomb Raiders.

Shohan gasped when he felt someone grab his hands behind him and secure them with a rope.

"Jaime!" He yelled when another masked man hit his colleague's head with the end of his rifle and the latter collapsed on the ground. It was not long before he felt a hijacker taped his mouth shut, rifle pointed at his chest.

Shohan helplessly watched the hijackers removing items from the lab. The skeletons were left untouched. Vases, bowls, and many other items in silver and gold were swept into a black duffle bag.

He whimpered. He was scared. He thought if this was how he was going to die, in the hands of tomb raiders. The last thing he saw was a man pocketing the body chain, which Bentley had found before he was knocked unconscious.

When he woke, he was in the back of a van. Jaime was still lying unconscious across from him. There was no window and he did not know where they were heading. An armed guard sat with them at the back of the van. Shohan briefly saw the body chain glittering from where it was spilling through the guard's pocket.

He knew it was a dangerous and stupid move. He scooted closer to the guard, pretending he was just wanting to get closer to Jaime.

"Mmmm! Mmmm!" Shohan tried prodding Jaime with his

foot.

The guard clicked his rifle and pointed straight at him and he froze. He was shouting at him before he used the back of his rifle to slap him across the face.

Shohan fell face down and he could feel warm blood oozing out from his nose. Where he laid, he saw the body chain on the ground. The hijacker must have dropped it during the commotion. He pretended to slide back to Jaime who seemed to be writhing awake. With his hands tied to his back, he scooted further back and retrieved the body chain before the van halted suddenly and the back doors of the van burst open.

Sunlight spilled through the van and it blinded him momentarily.

Gunshots ricocheted in the air and he ducked down, covering Jaime's body with his. The armed guard had abandoned the van and more gunshots were fired outside.

Shohan did not know when he had started crying, his eyelashes and cheeks were wet. He was terrified and Jaime was not exactly waking up anytime soon.

A pair of arms curled around his waist and hoisted him out of the van. He tried to scream but he was settled on the hot pavement. Looking up, he saw the local police talking into his walkie-talkie. He heard several more gunshots fired at a van speeding off.

An ambulance arrived shortly after and both he and Jaime were taken to the hospital.

"What the fuck? Are you two okay? Oh my god, you guys gave us a scare!"

Layton was the first to run into their ward. Jaime was beside him with a small plaster on his temple.

Shohan was only left with scratches on his forehead and cheek which were now plastered. His wrists however were scabbed with dried blood from him trying to untie himself earlier. "Doctor said they are superficial." His voice came out shaky, he still had not gotten over the earlier scare.

He looked to Jaime who hurriedly sat down by the edge of his bed.

Shohan could not help as he started to cry. His hands were still trembling. "I was so scared."

Jaime and Layton tried to console the young archaeologist. "We are here now. You're okay." Jaime hushed and brushed away his tears. It was oddly comforting.

"Most of the gold and silver artifacts were stolen. Most of the hijackers got away too." Layton huffed angrily, ears reddening.

Jaime shook his head and patted Shohan's arm. "It is fine. So long no one got seriously injured."

Shohan wiped away his remaining tears. He was still shaken but he found comfort in his colleagues.

While Jaime handled the hospital paperwork, Layton helped him up. Afterwhich, they got into Layton's rented car and drove back to the hostel. He leaned his head against Jaime's shoulder while the latter soothed his arm comfortingly.

"I don't want you two at the excavation site or the research facility today," Layton instructed as he sent both men to their individual rooms. "Please, rest up."

Shohan nodded. He could not bring himself back to the desert today anyway.

He put aside the body chain he managed to take back from the tomb raider and changed out of his sand-coated attire and slipped into a fresh pair of boxers. Staring at the full-length mirror at his hotel, his eyes wandered down to his chest where a small mole was. He let his finger caress over the small birthmark while he recalled the conversation he had with Jaime.

Punctured vertebrae and a chipped rib. He had heard myths about moles and birthmarks being how one had died during their previous life. If said Prince was indeed him, and if the prince really was assassinated, that explained the mole on his chest. But what were the odds?

Shohan sat at the edge of his bed and palmed his temples. He winced when he accidentally brushed over his wound. The medication he took was also starting to take effect and he let the drowsiness take over.

1500 B.C

Khai was sitting by his mother's bedside.

His mother's health had worsened since the last time he saw her. Her lips were pale and chapped, her once beautiful and flawless skin now dry and dull.

Khai stayed by her side as royal physicians tended to her. He knew his mother's days were numbered, for she had not been able to get out of her bed for two moons.

"Mother, are you sure you have been taking the herbs as prescribed?" Khai was concerned if the royal physicians were skilled enough.

His mother smiled wearily. "I do, my son. It is nothing worrisome."

Khai sighed and gave his mother's hand a light squeeze.

"You have a Kingdom to run, Khai. Nari shall keep me company." His mother pried her hand off from him.

Khai, as much as he loathed the Princess, his wife, was relieved that at least his mother did not have to spend her days alone in her chambers. With Princess Nari keeping his mother company, it allowed more time for him to focus on his Royal duties and also more time with his Prince.

"Okay, mother," Khai stood and bent down to press a kiss to his mother's forehead. "Rest plenty."

At the throne room, Khai was glad that his Prince was there with him. Although the Waranian Prince did not interfere with his Royal duties, his company alone was sufficient. It made his days pass by faster.

Sometimes Khai would be alone in his study chamber busy with his work and his Prince would drop by once in a while.

Khai did not complain about putting off work for his Prince.

They made love in Khai's study chamber. They made love in the mess hall after servants were done clearing the tables. They made love in the drawing room. They made love in the sand dunes when Khai would bring his husband along for a hunt with his cheetah. So long there was a surface to bend over the prince, they made love.

His sexual escapades with his Prince did not deter him from running the empire, rather, he found the kingdom thriving under his reign. The city prospered, the monumental temple for his Prince, the Luxor Temple, was nearing its completion. The Nile flooded once more, fertilizing its soil and blessing the land with crops.

However, it was a short-lived moment before the Nile, once again, dried up a few moons after.

Sevrin stood by his husband's side, watching royal physicians and priests chanting words of blessings.

Khai had his jaw clenched tight watching the physicians applying rolls of linen over his mother's body. His mother was dressed in a beige robe with a silvery sheen. Her skin was powdered by her chambermaids and it brought life back to her features.

Sevrin felt his husband's hand tightened around him. The news of the Queen Mother's death hit the entire kingdom.

They placed his mother's mummified body into a silver pleated coffin, engraved with spells to ward off tomb raiders before loading the coffin into a granite sarcophagus.

Royal members and staff gathered in the Queen Mother's chambers to pay their final respects.

Khai approached his mother's sarcophagus and placed a hand on top of the lid. His mother may not have given him the childhood he wanted, but he was still his mother after all. "I'm sorry, mother. Journey forth to the netherworld and be joined with father."

With his command, servants heaved the granite sarcophagus with poles bearing on their shoulders. The journey to the Valley of the Kings under the scorching sun would take an entire day's trip.

Khai was about to mount his warhorse when he felt soft fingers curled around his hand. He turned to see his Prince's crestfallen eyes.

"Let me come with you, Khai," Sevrin said in his softest voice. It hurt to see his husband mourning for his mother's death.

Khai looked around to see chambermaids, guards, and his wife with their heads bowed. It warmed his heart to know that his Prince was willing to journey with him in this sweltering heat.

As much as Khai wanted to tell the prince to rest in his quarters and he would be back by evenfall, a part of him wanted his Prince by his side too. It was then that Khai realized that Prince Sevrin was not just his husband, he was his best friend, his confidant.

"Are you sure, my love?" Khai reached up to brush a lock of hair off the prince's eyes.

Sevrin nodded. "You need me."

That was it for Khai. He sucked in a deep breath and let his tears fall. He needed his Prince. For the first time in his life, he needed someone, and that someone was finally there for him.

He let his arms wrap around his husband, showing him his most vulnerable side. "Thank you, my Prince." Khai peeled himself off and placed a long kiss on his husband's forehead. "What would I do without you…"

Sevrin was holding back a sob. It was the first time he saw Pharaoh Khai's tears. "You will be okay. I am here."

Khai brushed his palms against the prince's soft cheeks. "Come," Khai said and hoisted his Prince onto his warhorse before mounting behind him.

They watched the servants heaving the granite sarcophagus in front of them while they followed behind. Guards, including Kafre, rode around them with spears on hand.

As much as Sevrin hated the hot afternoon sun, he did not regret coming along with Pharaoh Khai. While Khai controlled Zohar's reins, he would occasionally rest his head on his shoulder. Sevrin would turn around and leave a chaste kiss on Pharaoh Khai's cheek or reach over to squeeze his arm.

By sundown, they reached the Valley of the Kings. This place was far from the palace and the night wind was cold against his skin. His husband helped him to dismount. The guards tethered their horses while servants heaved the granite sarcophagus into the tomb.

Khai, along with his husband, and the high priestesses from Karnak Temple, followed behind his mother's coffin.

The chamber's entrance was so narrow that Sevrin had to hunch to walk in while Pharaoh Khai had a hand protectively held above his head.

In the burial chamber, they oversaw the funerary procession. Sevrin never once let go of Khai's hand as they watched the priests chanting religious scriptures. He learned that the Egyptians believed that after their death, magical spells were needed to help them journey to the underworld where they would continue to rule the Kingdom. Servants also brought in the Queen Mother's most treasured items that were said to help her thrive in her afterlife.

After everyone had left his mother's burial chamber, he took his time to pay his final respects.

"I want to take you somewhere, Prince Sevrin," Khai turned to his Prince.

Sevrin was confused. "Where?"

Khai took his Prince's hand and guided him out of his

mother's tomb. When they were finally back in the desert dunes, Khai commanded his remaining servants and priests to leave. Kafre stayed behind.

Sevrin let himself be guided by Pharaoh Khai. They did not venture far before his husband led him towards another creak in the same Valley on the other side. "Where are you taking me, my King?"

Khai, as usual, held a protective hand above his Prince's head as they made their way into another narrow shaft.

Sevrin was enamoured. The chamber was strewn with gold statues and furniture. He turned back to the Pharaoh, confused.

"This is where I will be laid to rest when my time comes," Khai explained, he watched his Prince's expression fall, chest heaving.

Sevrin shook his head. "Please, my King. Do not speak of such words." He could not help letting his tears fall. Sevrin could never imagine not having his husband with him. It pained him to even imagine it.

"My Prince. I just want to tell you, I do not trust everyone in the palace," Khai spoke tenderly to his husband with both hands cupping his soft cheeks. "Not everyone knows where my resting place is."

Sevrin gazed up at Pharaoh Khai through his wet lashes. "What are you talking about, Khai?"

Khai sighed, gazing into his Prince's soft brown orbs. "I want you to know if you ever need to find a safe place. Come here, I will find you here."

Sevrin was not sure what his husband meant exactly. Maybe he was too tired, having to deal with his royal duties while mourning for his mother's death was not easy. Maybe he just needed some rest, he surmised.

"Please, promise me?" Khai asked again. He knew the palace was no longer a safe place. He needed to protect his Prince.

Sevrin nodded, "I promise."

CHAPTER 15

Present Day

After a much well-rested night, the young archaeologist found himself fit to go about. He took off the bandages on his temple and cheek since he was not bleeding anymore. His wrists, however, still spotted pink and lined with scabs.

He walked over to his nightstand and pulled out the body chain. He let it fall over his fingers and watched the way the rubies and quartz barbell dazzle.

Shohan wondered how the Pharaoh would take the news if he showed him this. He filed that thought away as he made his way to the hostel lobby and flagged for a cab. He needed to go back to the lab and work out the DNA sequence of the hair.

"Please, please, come on..." he muttered as the final report was being generated.

He looked them through, comparing all three sets of DNA, especially the fetal skeleton.

"But how..." he furrowed his brows at the results. The fetal skeleton had both the Prince and the Pharaoh's DNA. It was not possible for males to conceive. The limestone walls also stated that the Pharaoh had no heir. So, who was this baby?

He needed immediate answers. He needed to see the Pharaoh.

Shohan packed away the results. He had no idea how to answer anyone about the hair specimen. Nobody must find out about his research until he's certain.

Tunnels, narrow shafts, and more twists and turns down the chamber, Shohan found himself standing by the archway of the burial chamber, only this time, fire torches were already lit and he spotted the Pharaoh looking up at a particular engraved hieroglyph, hands clasped on his back and the young archaeologist almost ogled at his back muscles if the Pharaoh had not turned around.

Words he wanted to speak got caught in his tongue when the Pharaoh smiled and made a beeline for him.

Shohan watched the way the Pharaoh's eyes roamed over him before they became crestfallen again. He felt warm fingers ghosting over his cheek, just shy from his wound.

Pharaoh Khai then placed his other hand over his other cheek, eyes examining his cut temple that he knew was bruising.

"Who. Did this. To you."

He shuddered at how authoritative Pharaoh Khai sounded, he could almost feel the rage radiating from the King.

He blinked a couple of times, trying to find his voice. "I… I was—"

The archaeologist held his breath when Khai closed the distance, jaw clenched tight, his biceps clad in gold tautened when he clenched his fists. "Who hurt you!"

Shohan shut his eyes and swallowed when the Pharaoh raised his voice. He felt fear, his lips trembled as he tried to form coherent words. "Tomb… tomb raiders. They took me and my friend. They…" he trailed off, he did not know when he started to cry. The memory of being kidnapped and having a rifle gun pointed at him still traumatized him.

He was almost on the verge of breaking down but when he felt a pair of strong arms wrapped around him, his face pressed into the Pharaoh's warm chest, Shohan felt safe, he felt protected. Khai had a hand cupping the back of his head and he reveled in his embrace. Part of him did not want the King to let go.

"I will make them pay. Those who hurt you have to meet my wrath."

The Pharaoh's words resonated through his chest and the arms around him tightened. Shohan did not know what the words meant but at that moment, with the Pharaoh holding him tight, nothing else mattered.

When they broke apart, he felt Khai raise his hand and brushed off his remaining tears with his thumbs.

"Do not fear, my Prince…"

Shohan watched the way the Khai's eyes softened with every brush of the latter's palm on his wet cheeks. His breath was taken away.

"No harm shall come before you."

He dipped his head and curled his bottom lip between his teeth. He would be lying if he said his heart was not fluttering like a wild bird in his chest. He knew the Pharaoh loved the prince, but the prince was not him, at least not in this lifetime.

"I have something to say," Shohan peeked up through his wet lashes, he was not sure how to break the news to the Pharaoh. There was never a good time to deliver such heart-wrenching news anyway, but he had to. Khai needed his closure and his excavation time was running short. "Will you promise to stay? Please don't disappear on me again. You need to know this."

Pharaoh Khai pressed his lips into a tight line. He reached down and took hold of the archaeologist's hand and splayed it against his chest.

Shohan let his hand stay on the Pharaoh's chest as he watched him close his eyes and take a deep breath.

When Khai opened his eyes again, he saw the King's kohl-lined eyes were calm, no longer bloodshot. The Pharaoh nodded.

"My team and I might have found the prince you are looking for." He held his breath after finishing his sentence.

Pharaoh Khai's eyes widened and were once again filled with guilt, sorrow, and agony. "Take him to me, please…"

"I took a part of him here, to you," Shohan reached into his pocket and curled his fingers around the coolness of the body chain. He hesitated.

"Where did you find him? My Prince..."

His chest tightened at how hurt the King's voice sounded. He slowly pulled out the rubied body chain with a quartz barbell and presented it before the Pharaoh.

Pharaoh Khai held his breath, eyes boring into the piece of elegant jewellery on the archaeologist's hand.

Shohan thought the Pharaoh found the body chain familiar, his breaths coming out erratic, and tears pooled at the corner of his kohl-lined eyes.

Pharaoh Khai grabbed the body chain from him, holding it close to his chest, and lowered himself onto the ground, kneeling.

"Oh, my Prince. My Prince!" The Pharaoh's sorrowful cries echoed around the burial chamber. "Where have you gone... Why... why did you go..."

He squatted down to meet the Pharaoh's height, the latter's shoulders were trembling as he cried and cried, clenching the body chain close to his chest.

"We... found his remains not far from your tomb."

Pharaoh Khai then gazed up at him, eyes red and the kohl around his eyes was slightly smudged. "He was here? In the Valley of the Kings?" The Pharaoh looked hopeful for a moment as he stared into the archaeologist's eyes.

Shohan thought there were some things the Pharaoh was not telling him. He saw recognition in Khai's eyes and part of him was glad he had not disappeared. He nodded. "We... we also found the bones of a... feline."

Tears streaked down the Pharaoh's cheeks. He did not seem as anguished as he did when Shohan first met him. "He was not alone..."

That sounded more like the Pharaoh was talking to himself.

"There was also... one more thing," Shohan added, he felt uncertain. How would he explain to Khai? He would not understand modern language, what more a scientific report?

The Pharaoh's eyes were eager. He was no longer shedding tears, in fact, he looked calm and hopeful.

"The prince was with... a child..."

Tears welled up in the Pharaoh's eyes and he shook his head. "That is not..." he stood up, body chain clenched in one hand as he walked towards his golden coffin, shoulder tensed and heaving. "So, it was true... my Prince... my dear Prince..."

Shohan watched the Pharaoh muttering to himself. He was confused at how the Pharaoh was handling the information. He had expected the late King to cause an uproar and disappear.

The archaeologist stood up and slowly closed the distance. He reached out a hand and wrapped it around the Pharaoh's wrist that was holding onto the body chain. "Khai. I am sorry for your loss."

He felt the Pharaoh's tendons tautened under his touch.

When the Pharaoh did not speak, he let go of his hand and took a step back. He figured the Pharaoh needed his time to grieve, to come to terms with his loss. Shohan sighed and dipped his head. He had his back turned towards the Pharaoh and started to leave. For the first time, Khai did not stop him.

"Dr. Shohan, I heard what happened," Bentley said as he

packed artifacts into boxes that were to be transported to the research facility. "You don't have to come back to the research facility, Dr. Jaime will remain here at the site."

He smiled at his intern. "I am fine, Bentley."

Bentley sighed and turned to face him, arms folded in front of his chest. "I am saying, spend some time with Dr. Jaime here. Give the man a chance, Dr. Shohan."

Shohan only chuckled and brushed it off. He continued to pack the artifacts until Layton and Jaime ran into the tent, panting.

Both he and his intern exchanged looks.

"We got a call from the local police. They found the tomb raiders' van. We are called to retrieve the artifacts they had stolen." Layton said.

The archaeologist pinched his brows together. "How did they find the van?"

Jaime seemed shaken. "The police found the van five hours away from where they found us. The van flipped."

Shohan let out an inaudible gasp. "What about... them?"

"The tomb raiders? None of them survived," Layton added. "Bentley, you'll come with me. You two wait for us in the lab."

He was left in a daze. He remembered the words Pharaoh

Khai said.

I will make them pay. Those who hurt you have to meet my wrath.

He shuddered. Does that mean that Pharaoh Khai possessed powers? That Pharaoh Khai and the other previous reigning monarchs now rule Egypt in their afterlife in the netherworld?

"Come on, Shohan. Let's head back to the lab."

1500 B.C

Sevrin was in Pharaoh Khai's study chamber, with Horus perched on the window shaft while Jafaar laid by his feet.

After the death of the Queen Mother, Sevrin felt that he needed to offload some work from his husband. So, he decided to learn about the country's politics with the Pharaoh's court officials.

Khai did not mind. It kept his Prince company while he went on with his duties as a King. He was even looking forward to one day ruling the empire with his Prince.

When he was done with his duties at the throne room, Khai proceeded to the Great Hall for dinner with his guards following close behind.

He saw that the seat beside his golden throne was empty. He then took his seat beside Princess Nari. Dinner was mostly quiet, for everyone was still mourning for the Queen Mother.

He spotted Kafre entering the Great Hall without his Prince. Khai became concerned.

"Where is Prince Sevrin, Kafre?" Khai bit into his meat, watching his husband's personal guard picking up a tray with a golden plate towards him.

Kafre began picking out dishes. "His Highness is still in your study chambers. He said he will have his dinner there."

Khai sighed. As much as he was happy knowing the prince was learning about the country's politics to lighten his load, he did not like the idea of him skipping his meals.

"I shall take my leave, my King," Kafre bowed with a tray of food.

Khai nodded and dismissed Kafre.

"Are you not worried about the prince spending too much time with that bastard?"

He heard his wife mutter. He rolled his eyes. The Princess

and he never saw eye to eye. Khai was too exhausted to retort, but that said, his wife's words dampened his mood.

"It is a pity his mother was just a lowly chambermaid," Nari added, smacking her lips after taking a sip of mulled wine.

Khai had his fists clenched tight around his fork and he slammed his fist into his plate, the golden fork stabbed through his plate of meat. Gasps around the table were heard, priests, physicians, and some court officials in the Great Hall had not heard of their conversation but they were taken aback by his temper. Khai was rarely upset during dinners.

He did not like people belittling his guard. True to the Princess' words, Kafre was a chambermaid's son. His mother's personal chambermaid to be exact. He grew up with him and played with him. His mother had sent Kafre away when he was seven to train with the Assyrians, and when Kafre returned at sixteen years old, his mother announced Kafre as his personal guard, and the two had even fought countless battles and won wars together for the next few years. Kafre had kept him safe. Khai will forever remember the scar down Kafre's face for shielding him from the enemies.

"You do not speak of Kafre like this! He is a loyal guard who served the military and protected our country." He beseeched. Khai stood up so violently that his throne was knocked over. He no longer had an appetite.

He heard someone clearing his throat and looked up.

"Your Highness," Kafre entered the study and placed the tray of food before him.

His stomach belched at the smell of fish meat and he lightly pushed his tray away from him.

"Pharaoh Khai seemed worried that you were not present in the Great Hall," Kafre walked around the chamber, admiring the engraved scriptures on the walls and paintings on the ceilings. He was never taught to read or write, for his social status did not allow him to. He did not complain, he knew he was never in the position to, and when the Queen Mother had sent him off to Assyria, he never felt more in place. He was good with spears and swords, he also took great pride in his duty now as a guard.

Sevrin faintly smiled and rolled up the dried cow and sheepskin, placing them in a pile to be read tomorrow. He had lots to read and study.

"He is just overworked. I am not a child he has to worry about," Sevrin chuckled and pulled his tray of food closer. He scooped the fish meats aside, for the smell made him nauseous.

Kafre let out a hearty laugh. "Oh, I have known the Pharaoh since we were children. If my calculations were correct, he is now on his way up here."

Sevrin chortled. He loved Kafre's presence. He was like a friend to him, it made his days in Egypt less lonely when his husband was doing his duties as a King— taking a trip to the monumental temples to make sure works are well on their way, to the high temple of Karnak to pay his respects to the Gods and Deities and many more. It was difficult to even catch a glimpse of Pharaoh Khai during the day.

"I did not know that you grew up with the Pharaoh," Sevrin said with interest. "Tell me about you and him."

Kafre was about to speak but he halted when they heard approaching footsteps. He threw the Waranian Prince a knowing look and the young Prince broke out into a series of giggles when the Pharaoh stepped through the archway.

Khai looked back and forth between his husband and Kafre, eyebrows quirked up questioningly. "What did I miss?"

Kafre huffed out a sigh, clearly, his duties were dismissed now that the Pharaoh was here with the prince. "The only thing you missed, is His Highness," Kafre cocked his head towards the young Prince and smirked at his King.

"You little—"

Kafre was already out of his study chambers before Khai

could argue.

No matter how tired his eyes were from reading, from listening to the court officials giving him a lecture on politics, the sight of Pharaoh Khai before him was everything he needed.

"My Prince…" Khai leaned over his study table and captured the prince's soft lips with his own. He sighed after breaking off the kiss, forehead leaning against his husband's. "I have missed you."

Sevrin giggled when Pharaoh Khai let their noses brush. "That I have heard, from Kafre."

Khai's heart fluttered at the prince's playfulness. "So cocky." His eyes darted down to his husband's tray of untouched food. "Have you not eaten? Unwell, perhaps?"

Sevrin shook his head and sent Pharaoh Khai a reassuring smile. "It is not that. I think it is the hot weather getting to me. I just have no appetite."

Khai folded his arms in front of his chest as he studied his Prince. His husband was glowing, cheeks tinted pink and his skin looked smoother than ever. "No more visits to the city for now. I want you to rest plenty."

Sevrin's heart sank and he pouted. He loved visiting Thebes, he loved playing with the children, their smiles and laughter reminded him of his childhood back in Warania with his brother. It was like a little piece of home to him.

"And no more studying. You do not have to, my Prince."

Khai began taking away the rolled dried cow skins.

"But my King, I am now your husband," Sevrin stood up and walked up to Pharaoh Khai. He splayed his palm against his husband's chest, his fair skin stood out in contrast to the King's bronze chest which glimmered. "It is my duty to share your burdens."

Khai sighed and shook his head slightly, wrapping his arms around Prince Sevrin's lean waist. He gazed into his soft orbs and felt his breath taken away. His Prince had never looked more beautiful. "Oh, my beautiful, how lucky am I to have you," he released a hand from his waist to brush a lock of hair that was falling over his eyes. "But I do not want you to overwork yourself with such matters. Just you being with me is more than I can ever ask for."

Sevrin sighed, closing his eyes, and rested a side of his face against his Pharaoh's chest, listening to the strong heartbeat that was increasing with each moment. "But I want to, Khai."

Khai bit down on his bottom lip. He loved that his Prince was going out of his way for him. He also felt blood rushing down south with his husband's face on his chest. They had not been intimate since the passing of his mother. "I would love to bend you over my table but I also am in need of a bath." He groaned when he felt his Prince pushing his own hips against his half-hard cock.

"The bathing chamber is more comfortable if you ask me," Sevrin admitted bashfully, his own cheeks heating up.

Khai groaned in frustration. With Horus perched on the prince's shoulder and Jafaar by his side, Khai had never walked to his bathing chamber that fast in his life.

Khai had the chambermaids draw up a hot bath. He commanded Jafaar to stay guard at the archway of his bedchamber.

"Do not let me wait too long, my Prince," Khai crooned in a low whisper and left for the bathing chambers. He knew his husband needed more time to take off and put away his body chain.

Khai let the warm water loosen the tight knots in his muscles, head resting back against the curb as his chambermaids continued to throw in rose petals and premium bath salts into his bathwater.

He heard faint footsteps and craned up to see his Prince, all in his naked glory, walking towards the opposite side, limp cock swaying with every step, before lowering himself into the water. His own cock stirred when the prince let out a gasp, his skin beneath started to pink from the hot water.

Khai then reached underwater and stroked his half-hard cock, mouth slightly parted when he thumbed over his slit.

He watched his husband dipped underwater, ripples reaching him and splashed over his shoulders. Khai did not see his Prince resurface, water ripples, however, kept washing up against him.

"Oh fuck!" Khai threw his head back when he felt his Prince's soft lips wrapped around his cock. With both hands now underwater, Khai palmed his husband's soft cheeks, feeling the shape of his own cock against the hollow of the prince's cheek.

Khai parted his lips again and let out a dragged-out moan, which echoed around the walls of the bathing chamber. He tilted his head towards the chambermaids, who were still filling up the bathwater with rose petals. "Leave us," he hissed and the chambermaids clambered to leave.

Khai dragged two fingers under the prince's chin, urging him to resurface.

"Oh!" Sevrin sucked in lungfuls of air and climbed to straddle Pharaoh Khai. He was still catching his breath when his husband reached over and palmed his ass cheeks.

"I do not want you drowning," Khai whispered over the shell of his ear and felt his Prince keened under his touch, face buried in the crook of his neck.

Sevrin blushed as he straightened up and held Pharaoh Khai's face with his hand, his thumb ghosting over his prominent cheekbones. "You taste like rose," Sevrin bit down on his bottom lip, he knew his husband loved it when he talked like this and sure enough, he felt Pharaoh Khai's cock twitch against his perineum.

"You shall be the death of me," Khai sighed and smashed their lips together.

CHAPTER 16

1500 B.C

Silver sunrays spilled through the window shaft of the bedchamber. Sevrin shifted under the eiderdowns, his hand ghosting over where his husband should be. He opened his eyes groggily and was not surprised to see his husband not here with him.

The sun hung high in the sky, it must be midday, he thought.

He heard a soft purr before a huge silhouette of a feline leaped onto his bed and nudged his waist with its nose. Sevrin giggled and reached over to scratch Jafaar's favourite spot behind its ear. When Jafaar laid down and rested its head on his chest, Sevrin hissed and moved away from the feline. His nipples were oddly tender, he did not remember Khai paying much attention to them when they made love last night. He was also still slightly tired even though it was already midday.

"I will get you some raw meat from the cook," Sevrin muttered to Jafaar and threw his eiderdowns aside. He walked towards the full-length mirror and blushed at the number of bruises that had blossomed between his thighs and along his collar bones. His skin felt surprisingly smooth and he thought he was glowing.

Sevrin fetched his shoulder sash robe from the drawer and dressed up. He commanded Jafaar to follow him unleashed.

"Your Highness."

Kafre was standing guard outside the bedchamber who was eyeing Jafaar warily. "Good morning, Kafre."

"It is midday, Your Highness," Kafre bowed to him with a smirk. "I see the Pharaoh had kept you up all night."

Sevrin blushed and dipped his head down. He cleared his throat before looking up at his personal guard trying to stifle a laugh. "I need to fetch some raw meat from the cook."

Kafre gave Jafaar a pointed look. "I am certain I would have torn the falcon to pieces if I were him."

Sevrin's jaw fell slack and Kafre let out a hearty laugh.

"Come. I know a shortcut to the kitchen," Kafre started leading but halted suddenly.

Sevrin walked right into Kafre and winced at how tender his body was, almost everywhere felt sore.

"But do not tell anyone. I sometimes sneak into the kitchen to steal some sweetmeats," Kafre said with a playful smile hanging on his lips.

Sevrin wondered if Pharaoh Khai and Kafre were often up to mischief in the palace when they were children.

When they reached the kitchen, cooks were brewing huge pots of pottage, some were kneading dough while the others tended to the fire oven. One side of the kitchen stank of raw meat and his stomach did a flip but he swallowed it in.

Kitchen staff bowed to him, fear clouded their eyes when they saw the King's pet cheetah beside him.

Kafre led him to the furthest end where a kitchen cook was knifing through a goat, blood spilled onto the floors. Sevrin kept his eyes away from the bloodied floors and walked on. The stench of poultry and fish meat mixed in the air did it for him as Sevrin clenched his hand around his stomach and ran for the nearest garderobe and threw up his stomach's contents.

He felt rough hands rubbing up and down his spine.

"Your Highness, do you want me to fetch a royal physician?"

Sevrin wiped his mouth with the back of his hand, still gasping for breath. He nodded wearily. His knees were so weak that Kafre had to pull him up. "Do not tell the King of this. He will worry." Sevrin threw Kafre a worried look.

Kafre huffed out a sigh and nodded. "I will get the raw meat for Jafaar," he offered the Waranian Prince a goblet of water. "Head back to the bedchamber, I shall fetch a physician for you, Your Highness."

Sevrin gladly took the goblet and downed its contents. He patted his thigh and Jafaar followed him obediently. He took a turn and walked to his own chambers instead.

"I thought you would be in the King's chambers, Your Highness," Kafre stood by the prince's bedchamber archway with a physician behind him. "I have been searching for you."

Sevrin sat up and scooted back till he could rest against the golden headboard. "I apologize, I did not want Khai to worry."

Kafre let himself in and motioned for the physician to enter. "This is Atum, I shall leave you some privacy. I will be outside, call if you need me, Your Highness."

Sevrin nodded.

The physician, Atum, had a head of white hair. He looked like he had served the royal family before Pharaoh Khai was even born.

"Please lay down, Your Highness."

Sevrin laid down as Atum knelt before the edge of his bed and took his hand, two fingers lightly applying pressure to his wrist's pulse point. He watched Atum's eyebrows slowly furrowed together, head cocking to one side as if he was reading his pulse like a language.

Atum then placed his wrinkled hand against his forehead. "Have you been taking your meals regularly, Your Highness?"

"I did not have much appetite for some time," Sevrin said, which was true, he had not eaten much, and more recently, he had never fully finished a meal.

Atum released his hand on his wrist and placed both hands underneath his jaw, lightly applying some pressure as if he was looking for something. Atum shook his head.

"It is not an infection. Your lymph nodes are not swollen," Atum sighed in concern. "When did you start experiencing loss of appetite?"

Sevrin counted in his head and hummed in thought. "Since the Queen Mother's passing?"

"Have you been visiting the garderobe more frequently?"

Sevrin saw uncertainty in the physician's eyes. "Yes, I kept waking up at night too."

Atum mumbled something indecipherable.

He slowly sat up and winced at how his lower back felt sore.

Atum seemed to have noticed. "Do you feel unwell in other areas?"

Sevrin nodded. "I feel… sore. Everywhere." He hoped the physician did not need him to strip off his robes. He did not want anyone to know of the bruises Khai left on him.

Atum looked at him in disbelief. "This is not possible…" the physician shook his head.

Sevrin was starting to panic. Did he catch some unknown and deadly disease? Was he going to die?

"Atum. What is it?" He hugged his knees to his chest, suddenly feeling small and frail.

Atum sucked in a shaky breath. "I apologize in advance, Your Highness, but may I ask if there was someone or something you had come across? Something nobody speaks of, something nobody would understand if you said so?"

Sevrin had his brows pinched together, he did not understand what the physician was trying to say. He shook his head.

"I have heard word going around that Your Highness visits the city of Thebes often. Could you perhaps … have visited someone or somewhere you should not have?"

Sevrin was starting to get impatient. "I do not understand

a word you speak of."

"Dark spells, Your Highness…"

He watched the physician tremble in his spot as if he had feared him. "I still do not understand?"

Atum looked at him and swallowed. "It seems to me that you are… with child, Your Highness. Every symptom you described, and I felt two sets of pulses on you."

Sevrin shook his head. "It is not possible. I am a man. Men do not conceive."

Atum bowed, he was heaving, chest rising and falling. He nodded and said, "You are right, Your Highness, but man can conceive if dark spells were cast upon them. I have seen it with my own eyes. Many, many years ago before the Pharaoh was even born."

Sevrin's jaw fell slack, he tried to say something but his mind could not form words.

"If my diagnosis and presumptions were true," Atum reached into his sash and pulled out two seeds. "Urinate on the seeds. If the black one sprouts, you are carrying a boy. If the green one sprouts, you are carrying a girl. If none sprouts, then you are not with child."

Sevrin reached out with his palm open, watching Atum place the seeds on his hand.

"I will not speak a word to anyone about this," Atum stood

up and was about to leave.

Sevrin grabbed his hand and a tear streaked down his cheek. "If I am," he swallowed thickly, finding his voice. "Will I survive it?"

Atum gave him a faint smile. "You will, Your Highness. But it has to be done in secrecy."

"Is… is this child… even mine?" He choked back a sob. He could not imagine having a living thing growing in him, let alone a child that was not his.

"It is as much your child as it is to the Pharaoh. Such spells only work if intercourse happens." Atum explained.

Sevrin sniffled and nodded.

"You can call for me whenever you need, Your Highness. I shall see to it that no harm comes to you and your child till it is born." Atum reassured him with a squeeze on his hand. Somehow, Atum seemed like a fatherly figure to him. "Urinate on the seeds. It will sprout overnight."

"Thank you, Atum." He said and watched as the physician gave him a sympathetic smile and left.

Sevrin curled his arms around his belly. A child. What would Khai think of him? Would Khai be disgusted that he's an abomination? Who would believe that he's carrying a child?

Sevrin curled into a fetus position, one arm resting on his belly as he cried into his pillow. Jafaar leaped onto the bed when he heard his cries. Sevrin stroked the feline's fur as he continued to let tears fall. "What do I do, Jafaar… what is happening to me…"

"It has to be done, my King."

Khai paced about his study chamber. Court officials, guards, and priests gathered for the one and only remaining problem his country was facing.

The Nile River.

It had been almost two years since the Nile dried. Farmers could not put bread on their table, for their soil had not been able to produce crops. The mortality rate had increased especially in infants and the homeless. Crime rates had also increased with famine on the rise.

The building of temples and monuments had not improved the city's situation either.

Agafya and other priests had suggested a sacrificial trip.

Khai sighed, hands rested against the window shaft looking out to Thebes. It must be done.

"Ready the men, horses, camels, and sacrificial herds. We leave at first light tomorrow." Khai reluctantly instructed.

"Yes, my King." The priests and guards said in unison and filed out of his study chamber.

Khai dismissed his court officials. His personal guard who replaced Kafre stayed behind, along with Plato.

"Please tell me I am done for the day." Khai exhaled tiredly. He needed to spend more time with his Prince. He had to leave by first light and the sacrificial trip would take several moons, for he would have to travel down the Nile by camels, who were sacred animals that were said to bless the Nile with water if a royal King rode down the Nile to Aswan, the endpoint of his trip.

Plato bowed and said, "Of course, my King. They are not a worry for now."

Khai nodded. "Rasiff."

His personal guard stepped forth. "Yes, my King?"

"Oversee the preparation of the guards who will come

along. I shall be in my chambers. Be ready at first light."

Khai's heart thumped worriedly in his chest. His chamber was empty, his Prince's chest of jewelleries and body chains were not here either. He rushed over to the closet to see that his Prince's Waranian robe was also gone.

"Kafre!"

Khai's voice resonated through the palace walls. He searched Jafaar's dungeon and the feline was not there. He was starting to get worried until he heard familiar heavy footsteps.

"You called for me, my King?"

Khai turned to see a confused Kafre, sword safely sheathed by his waist. "Where is Prince Sevrin?"

"In his chambers?" Kafre quirked up a brow at him.

Still, it did not put his mind at ease. He had to see his husband right away.

"My Prince?" Khai strode past the archway to find his husband resting on his bed with Jafaar laying protectively beside him with its head resting on the prince's belly. The sight was endearing and Khai wanted to jump into bed to join his Prince if it wasn't for the fact that his husband was sleeping so peacefully. It eased his worries knowing that Jafaar had not only warmed up to Prince Sevrin but also was protective of him.

Khai slowly sat himself down beside his Prince. Jafaar's eyes slowly opened to reveal his bright ivory orbs, seeing that there was no threat, his cheetah closed its eyes and let the rise and fall of the prince's belly lull him back to sleep.

It knifed his heart to see the prince's under eyes slightly pink and puffy. Had his husband been crying?

Khai gently swept a lock of hair and tugged it behind the shell of the prince's ear. He then cupped his calloused hand on his cheek, feeling the warmth and softness of his skin. His husband stirred.

Sevrin stretched and almost jolted upright when he felt someone lying beside him. "Khai?'

"Did I wake you?" Khai spoke delicately. He let his fingers curl by the prince's svelte waist before snaking his arm around, pulling him close to his chest.

Sevrin's breath hitched and a lump grew in his throat as he forced himself not to let tears spill once more. He shook his head, turning so that he could bury his face in Pharaoh Khai's warm chest.

Khai felt something was amiss, his Prince seemed unusually quiet. "Is something the matter?" Khai tilted his husband's chin up with two fingers.

Sevrin opened his mouth and gazed at his husband's warm orbs. "I… did Kafre say something to you?" He felt small as he spoke those words. Kafre had promised not to tell the Pharaoh that he was unwell, given their childhood relationship, he was uncertain if Kafre would tell the King. He recalled the words of Atum and now he felt like he could not trust anyone in the palace other than his husband.

"No. But why did you coop yourself up here? Did you not like being in my chambers?"

Sevrin shook his head. "I thought that I should give you some time to yourself, you have not really rested well since…" he trailed off. He did not like bringing up the topic of the Queen Mother but he had to lie. He was not sure how to break the news to his husband.

"But I do not like us to be apart every night." Khai laid down so that they could look each other in the eyes. He was worried about him. His Prince had not smiled since he stepped foot in the West Wing.

"Then sleep here." Sevrin let himself scoot closer to his Pharaoh and wrapped his hand around his waist. His husband's warm skin against his cheek was comforting.

Khai pressed a kiss to his Prince's forehead and sighed. "I am leaving at first light."

Sevrin immediately peeled away and propped himself up with an elbow. "Why are you leaving?"

Khai let out a pained smile and cupped his husband's face, "I have to make a sacrificial trip to Aswan. It will take several moons."

Sevrin felt selfish. He did not want him away for that long. "Then take me with you," he splayed a palm on Pharaoh Khai's chest and felt the latter let out a long exhale.

"It will be an exhausting journey. The desert will be scorching hot in the day and bitterly cold at night. I do not want you to fall ill."

Sevrin slumped back on the bed and let Pharaoh Khai hold him close. If he was indeed with child, he might not survive the harsh weather. He shut his eyes and took a couple of deep breaths. "I understand."

"It pains me to leave your side, my love," Khai let his palms sooth the prince's soft cheeks. He would miss him dearly when he's gone. "But I promise I will come back to you."

"And I will wait faithfully for you, my King."

Sevrin arose to an empty chamber and he sprang up immediately. The sun was still low beyond the horizon. He hurriedly put on his shoulder sash robe and sprinted to the foyer.

Horses, camels, herds of oxen, sheep, and goats were at the foyer, along with a group of guards.

"Khai? Khai!" Sevrin hugged his belly and looked around frantically.

"My Prince…" Khai pushed through the group of royal guards. He wrapped his husband in a tight embrace. He did not want to let go.

"I feared you had left," a single tear rolled down his cheek and he felt stupid for crying. Now he had definitely worried his King.

Khai felt his chest tightened. It warmed and pained him at the same time, for the prince did not want to see him go. "Not without seeing you," Khai leaned in and captured his Prince's soft lips. He could taste the saltiness of his husband's tears.

"I… I love you, Khai," Sevrin dipped his head shyly, this was the first time he had told his husband he loved him.

Khai swore if he was not about to leave for a sacrificial trip, he would have pulled his Prince to his own bedchamber and made love to him. Khai sighed and leaned his forehead against his Prince. "I love you too, my Prince. Please, rest and eat plenty. I will come back to you, it is a promise." Khai then pressed a long kiss on his Prince's forehead, down to the tip of his nose, and lastly, on his lips before he reluctantly peeled himself away and mounted on a camel.

Sevrin watched Pharaoh Khai reining his camel to stand. Guards mounted their horses and took their positions around their King while priests and servants ushered the herd of animals behind.

Another tear betrayed him as Sevrin ran forward. "Khai… Khai…."

Khai halted his camel, turning back to see his husband beside him again. He watched his Prince reach out a hand and a piece of jewellery glistened under the morning sun. It was the ruby necklace his husband had gifted him that was said to have the power to protect its wearer from all evils. He reached out and grabbed the necklace, their fingers brushed and Khai was holding back every ounce of energy from dismounting and calling off the trip.

"Please come back to me safely," Sevrin whispered.

Khai was now choking back on his own tears. He hated the Gods for testing his ability to rule the kingdom. At this very moment, Khai wished he was not a Pharaoh. He just wanted to be his Prince's husband.

Khai let his Prince take his hand and place it on his own cheek. He felt his husband leaning in for more warmth. "I will come back to you as soon as I can. That is my promise to you, my Prince." He let his thumb caress his husband's wet cheek.

Sevrin reluctantly let go of Pharaoh Khai's hand and watched him clasp the ruby necklace around his neck.

"We set forth now."

That was the last thing Sevrin heard his husband say before he watched Pharaoh Khai and his procession of guards, priests, and servants fade into the desert dunes.

CHAPTER 17

1500 B.C

They arrived at the city of Thebes. His people bowed to pay their respects to him. Khai briefly saw the boy in rags, Ufu, sleeping peacefully in his mother's arms. The boy reminded him of his Prince. His heart was still in the palace. Khai tightened his hold on his camel's reins and willed away his thoughts of turning his camel around to head back to his husband.

They spent days under the scorching desert sun riding through cities and smaller villages. Nights were spent setting up tents in the desert dunes. His men were tired and so was he, but what kept Khai going was the thought of returning to his Prince at the end of the trip.

Once they reached the Nile, priests started blessing the soil they walked on where the river once flowed. Every day when the sun was set at its highest, a pair of livestock was sacrificed.

Tents were set while Khai took some time away from his men. Rasiff, his personal guard, never strayed far from him. Khai missed having Kafre as his guard, he imagined having hearty conversations with his best friend if he was here, it would have made his trip less agonizing but he knew that Kafre would keep his mind more at ease if he were to stay with his husband.

The sun was setting beyond the horizon and here in Aswan, the river was starting to fill, though it looked more like a tiny stream of water.

Khai was looking far out into the desert when he heard an unfamiliar voice speak beside him.

"A King's greed and selfishness will cause the downfall of his empire."

The voice was hoarse and deep, it did not sound like a human's voice. Khai turned to look. A man slightly shorter than him was dressed in a gunny sack cloak over his head and holding a wooden walking stick. His eyes were covered and shadowed by his cloak. He could see that his blackened lips were dried and peeling, his skin was wrinkled with open sores.

A Seer. An eternally damned being that still walked the earth.

Khai turned to see Rasiff looking at him calmly. His guard must not have been able to see the Seer.

"The Nile will flood once more. However, it will be filled with the blood of your people and your foes."

Khai clenched his fists tight. "Mind your words. It is the King you are speaking with." He spat.

He saw the Seer's blackened lips curled into a smirk and chuckled. "It is not my words. They are the words from the high Gods. I am just a conveyor, a messenger."

Khai kept mum. He knew the Seer could not harm him, he was not a sorcerer.

"A King in love is also a weak King."

That enraged Khai. "I am not a weak King! I, the Great Pharaoh of Egypt, had fought and won battles for my country. I have allies across lands and oceans. Do not speak words which you will regret."

Khai watched the cloaked Seer turn his back on him and walked.

"The day his feet touch the hot desert sand, will be the day he takes his last breath."

"One more word—" Khai shouted, hands balled into tight fists, and was about to throw a punch at the Seer but another voice interrupted him.

"My King, is something the matter?"

Khai turned to see Rasiff by his side, sword still packed safely in his scabbard by his waist. He frantically turned around.

The Seer was gone.

Present Day

Shohan was dusting the reclaimed artifacts with his junior intern while his two colleagues, Layton and Jaime, continued to transport the artifacts from the van outside the research facility.

"It is a pity that almost all of them shattered. It will take a long time for us to restore them." The young archaeologist sighed.

Bentley nodded, labelling a sticker onto a long table as he sorted out the broken pieces of porcelain by their colour. "We are lucky they did not take the skeletons. By the way, did you run the DNA test? Were they a match?"

Should he tell his team about the three sets of matching DNA? How was he supposed to explain where the hair came from? He had not exactly told them he had found Khai Tutankhamen's tomb. "They were. The adult and the child."

Bentley grew teary-eyed and Shohan could see the tip of his nose starting to pink.

"This...." Bentley had his face scrunched up as he tried to speak. "This is so... SAD!" The intern wailed and clutched a broken piece of blue porcelain to his chest.

"There we go again," Layton rolled his eyes at Bentley as he carried a box of retrieved artifacts into the lab. "These are all we managed to collect, most of them are broken though."

Jaime, however, stood by the sliding doors of the lab, eyes roaming around. "Did anyone see the body chain?"

Shohan pretended he did not hear his colleague. Taking an artifact from the research facility without permission was a crime in Egypt. He did not want to stay behind bars in a foreign country. He feigned ignorance as he pretended to analyse a piece of porcelain Bentley had laid out.

"Did the raiders even take it?" Layton gazed up and looked around too. "It could still be around here, somewhere. C'mon Jaime," Layton heaved loudly as he lifted another box onto the table. "I'm sure we will find it eventually. The body chain is not important now. Let's sort these out."

1500 B.C.

Sevrin kept to himself mostly. Jafaar never left his side. It was as if the feline could sense that he was with child and it sparked its protective instincts. The cheetah growled whenever people other than Kafre stood closer to him than they should.

Kafre had since learned about it. His belly was growing and he had started wearing his Waranian robe since it was baggy and less revealing than a royal Egyptian's shoulder sash robe.

He missed the Pharaoh dearly. It had been three moons since he last saw him. Kafre sat beside him while Jafaar laid by his feet. They were breaking fast in the Great Hall.

Princess Nari, who was a seat away from him, seemed to be in good spirits. She talked with the royal guards and court members while they ate.

"You seemed to have an appetite, Prince Sevrin?"

He turned to the smiling princess and back to his plate of food.

"You seemed to have put on some weight too. Cooping up in your chambers is not very healthy."

Sevrin felt his stomach belched, not from his food, but at the princess' words. He did not trust the Begonion Princess. "Thank you for your concern, Princess Nari. But it is nothing you should worry about."

He heard the princess scoff condescendingly.

"Kafre," Sevrin pushed away his half-eaten food. He was hungry, but he could not stomach being in the presence of the Begonion Princess.

"Yes, Your Highness?"

Sevrin stood up and Jafaar was immediately at his heel. "Take me to my chambers."

"Prepare a bath for the prince." Kafre gave out orders to the prince's chambermaids. He watched the Waranian Prince waddle towards the window shaft where he kept a pot of plant which had blossomed.

Sevrin let the blossomed flower linger under his nose as he took in a sniff. The seedling which he had urinated on moons ago, had sprouted and now had blossomed into a black rose. The green seed, however, never sprouted.

He placed a hand on his slightly swollen belly, feeling the slight movement of kicks. He wondered if the King would be delighted to know that he was giving him an heir.

"You are all dismissed," Sevrin said and his chambermaids hurriedly left. He peeled off his Waranian robe and stepped into the hot bath. The hot water eased his sore waist and swollen feet. He missed taking baths with his Pharaoh. He replayed the memories of Pharaoh Khai brushing his hair and him lathering up his King.

When he was done, he wrapped himself in his night robe and exited the bathing chamber towards his chest of jewelleries. He sighed frustratingly. He remembered having placed his pure gold body chain among his other jewelleries but he had not been able to find it. He decided to pick a silver body chain with diamonds embedded with a quartz barbell instead. After he hooked the barbell through his pierced navel, he turned to see Kafre feeding Jafaar cubes of raw meat by the archway. His stomach growled at the sight, he did not get to finish his breakfast earlier.

"I have ordered the guards outside not to let anyone come in," Kafre straightened up and wiped his hand on his black kilt.

"Thank you, Kafre." Sevrin settled himself on his study chair, watching Horus grooming its own broad wings.

Kafre sighed and leaned against one of the walls, looking at him. "Someone should know, Prince Sevrin."

Blood drained from his face and he gasped at what Kafre suggested. "No! No one else can learn about this." Sevrin subconsciously curled his hand protectively over his belly. "It is not safe."

"The Waranian King and Queen should know, at least, they will not harm you." Kafre strode towards him and Horus. "Write to them."

Sevrin thought for a while. Kafre was right, his own Mother and Father would not harm him. He suddenly had an idea and felt less afraid.

While Kafre kept Jafaar busy, Sevrin pulled out a sheet of dried sheepskin and began writing.

Mother, Father.

I am writing to inform you that Pharaoh Khai would be expecting an heir. I cannot reveal much in this missive, lest Horus gets intercepted.

I need to come home for a while. I need to stay in Warania until his heir is born. I cannot stay here in Egypt when Pharaoh Khai is away for a sacrificial trip to Aswan.

I will have my guard accompany me on the trip.

Sevrin.

Sevrin had Kafre fetch him rolls of dried sheepskin from Pharaoh Khai's study chamber. He tried to keep himself occupied by studying politics since he now could not go out to Thebes. His Waranian robe had so far kept his pregnancy a secret but he knew his belly was growing bigger each day. Atum, the royal physician, also visited his bedchamber every fortnight to check on his pulse and bring him herbal medicines since a male's body was not meant to carry a child.

Nights were hot and humid, and with his growing belly, it was difficult for him to fall asleep. He had grown used to falling asleep without Pharaoh Khai's arms around him. Sometimes, Sevrin woke up lonely, some nights, he cried himself to sleep.

Tonight, Sevrin was awakened by his growling stomach. He hugged his night robe tighter around his body, for the night was cold.

He needed to eat, if not, for his unborn child. He quickly wrapped himself up with his Waranian robe and quietly tiptoed out of his chamber. He did not want an excited cheetah by his feet in the dead of the night when everyone else was asleep.

"Oh!"

Sevrin halted at the voice. It was Kafre, who had sat himself down by the archway to keep guard. Sevrin felt guilty that his personal guard had to sleep on the cold granite floors.

"Why are you up, Your Highness?" Kafre stood up slowly, rubbing his eyes groggily.

"Sorry, did I wake you?" Sevrin then felt a soft kick in his belly and placed his hand where it kicked and it seemed to calm down his child. "I was hungry. I was about to go to the kitchen to fetch some sweetmeats."

Kafre then chuckled. "I shall bring them up to you, Your Highness. It is dark and the kitchen smells bloody."

Sevrin wrinkled his nose in disgust. He remembered throwing up his stomach's contents the last time he went to the kitchen to fetch Jafaar some raw meat. "Okay," he nodded.

Jafaar was still sleeping soundly on his bed as Sevrin slowly sat himself down and rid of his Waranian robe, one had curled on his belly while the other stroked the feline's fur.

Some time had passed and he began to hear approaching footsteps. He continued to stroke the cheetah's fur and said, "Thank you, Kafre. Please, sleep on the lounge chair. The floor is cold at night."

He heard a high-pitched chuckle and his heart jumped. Sevrin turned to see the Begonian Princess standing by his archway, eyeing his swollen belly. Sevrin pulled his night robe loose but it did not help cover.

"Inviting another man into your bedchamber while the Pharaoh is away?" Princess Nari scoffed, arms folded across her chest. Sevrin saw her chambermaids and two armed guards enter as well. "What will Pharaoh Khai think if he learns about this? That his oh, so beloved Prince, was sleeping with his most trusted guard?"

Sevrin shook his head, his nose tingled and his eyes blurred with tears. "It is not what you think it is!" He hissed.

He saw Nari lowered her gaze to his belly.

"And what would he think if he learns that his Prince is carrying a child? His child? Or Kafre's?" Nari laughed and Sevrin heard her own chambermaids chuckling among themselves. "To think your belly will go unnoticed by me?"

Sevrin was afraid. He heard a low growl before Jafaar leaped to stand guard in front of him, baring its sharp canines, its back curled and ready to attack.

"How is this possible? A man, carrying a child? An abomination. Pharaoh Khai will never acknowledge the monster you are carrying." Nari paced back and forth, smugness hung on her lips as she spoke.

Jafaar stayed by his side on high alert. Sevrin began crying, what if it was true, that he was indeed carrying a monster? Pharaoh Khai would never accept him, he would never love him again and that thought alone scared that wits out of him.

"I know you love the Pharaoh and he loves you just as much. If you do not wish for him to see you differently, leave." Nari's eyes narrowed on him. "Leave! And never come back!"

That was it for Sevrin. Without even grabbing his Waranian robe, Sevrin ran out of his chambers.

The desert sand was hot on his feet. He ran and ran until his legs could not carry him anymore. He ran towards the direction where Pharaoh Khai said would keep him safe.

The Valley of the Kings.

He would hide in Pharaoh Khai's future resting place where not many knew about. It was hard to run without proper footwear, he stumbled a few times and his feet were beginning to blister.

The wind was cold and Sevrin only had a sheer piece of night robe on. He heard the sound of feet against sand behind him and turned to see the silhouette of a cheetah growing bigger.

"Jafaar!" He cried and his knees buckled.

The feline circled around him before nuzzling his head on his face. He saw that a side of the cheetah's jaw was bloodied.

"What did she do to you!" Sevrin wailed and hugged the feline. He had to run, no, *they* had to run. He watched Jafaar stand up on all four legs before he crouched as if he was ready to leap.

Jafaar must have followed his scent in search of him. The Princess must have hurt Jafaar and the feline knew he had to keep him safe. He swung a leg over Jafaar's back and held onto him tightly.

Jafaar then stood up high and the both of them leaped into the desert dunes.

It was not long before Sevrin heard the sound of horses' hooves. He turned slightly to see a group of guards on their horses, bows, and arrows held high and aiming at both him and Jafaar.

He heard the hiss of the arrows shooting past them before they anchored on the desert sand. Jafaar's paws never stopped running.

Everything happened too fast. Jafaar let out a high-pitched whimper and they both stumbled onto the hot sand. Sevrin turned to see Jafaar limping with an arrow pierced through its thigh, the feline, however, held on to the pain and limped towards him, keeping close. Jafaar was nosing Sevrin, urging him to stand back up.

"Argh!" He heard a faint scream behind.

As he ran with Jafaar limping closely by his side, Sevrin turned to see a familiar figure on a horse with his broadsword. One of the Princess' guards had fallen onto the sand. It was dark but Sevrin could make out the dead body on the ground.

"Kafre!" He screamed, one hand holding onto his belly.

"Run, Prince Sevrin. Go!" Kafre shouted and reined his horse towards the other guards with bows and arrows.

Sevrin cried as he turned his back on his guard and ran with Jafaar limping close.

His sore feet could not carry him much further. Jafaar was falling behind but before Sevrin could turn, he felt a piercing pain through his chest. His knees buckled and he fell onto his side. Every breath hurt and he tasted blood in his mouth. His eyes looked towards the valley's creak, he was so near, he was almost there. He gazed down where an arrow pierced through his chest, blood was soaking through his robe.

"Get rid of the cat." He heard the familiar female voice.

Sevrin tried taking a breath but it only made him choke on his own blood. "Ja…." He winced at the pain and curled himself into a fetus position. Jafaar came into his view, it seemed like the feline was trying to limp towards him but before he could reach him, Sevrin saw an arrow pierced through Jafaar's chest and the feline dropped onto the ground an arm's length away from him. He heard a low ringing in his ears as his vision tunnelled. He looked back at the valley's creak and let the last of his tears fall. "Kh..ai…"

Clutching his belly tight, memories of him and his Pharaoh flashed before his eyes, words from his husband and his father replayed in his head.

He remembered the Pharaoh asking for his hand in marriage.

Will you marry me, Prince Sevrin?

He remembered the last time he hugged his father good-bye.

You are now a man, a Pharaoh's husband. And I am very proud of you, Sevrin.

He remembered the wedding with Pharaoh Khai and the very first night they made love.

I can wait for you but I cannot lose you, my Prince. I am now your family too.

He remembered the first time he went to Thebes with Kafre.

I see why the Pharaoh is so smittened by you, Your Highness. You have a big heart.

He remembered the day Pharaoh Khai dressed himself as a palace guard in Thebes. Though he was in great pain, he let out a faint smile.

He remembered when Pharaoh Khai brought him to his burial chamber which was not far from where he was now. Even with his tunnelling vision, Sevrin could still make out the small creek in the valley.

I want you to know if you ever need to find a safe place. Come here, I will find you here. Please, promise me?

A single tear rolled down his cheek. He had promised but he had failed to keep it. "I'm... sorry, ugh!" He winced when he tried to breathe, warm blood trickled down to his chin and cheek. "Khai...."

He remembered sending Pharaoh Khai off for his trip. He remembered their last kiss.

I will come back to you as soon as I can. That is my promise to you, my Prince.

He felt weak. The desert sand was hot on his skin but the wind was cold. Sevrin let out one final exhale and watched the valley's creak fade into a dark abyss.

CHAPTER 18

Present Day

Their time in Egypt was running short. Shohan's heart clenched at the thought of leaving, he felt as if he had unfinished business.

He spent the next few days with his team organizing the reclaimed artifacts and restoring them as much as they could. Vases, bowls, and other pottery were pieced together and encased in a sterile cabinet that was to be put up for display in the National Museum of Egypt.

"Hey, some of the team members are thinking of visiting the local temples," Jaime came up to him after they were done packing and cleaning up the lab allocated to them for their excavating project. "Word has it that Karnak Temple never let a prayer go unanswered. Do you wanna… come along?" Jaime stuttered, hand reaching behind his own nape, cheeks slightly blushing.

Bentley must have convinced his colleague to ask him out. "I have already visited Karnak temple with Bentley, I… think I want to go back to the tomb. I don't want to give up just yet even though we are returning today."

Jaime's disappointment was evident across his face. "Do you want me to... come with you?" He offered, his tone still sounding dejected.

Shohan placed a hand on his shoulder, giving it a light squeeze. "It is fine. Go visit the temples, they are absolutely beautiful. Here," he reached into his backpack and retrieved a small notebook. "I had most of the hieroglyphs translated when I visited the temples, I had also indicated where these translations belonged in each temple."

Jaime brightened up and Shohan felt less guilty for having turned down the man.

His team had always depended on him for the translation of hieroglyphs, he only hoped that when they returned to Egypt next time, he would be able to uncover the truth to them; about Khai Tutankhamen's tomb and his lost Prince.

"Thank you, Shohan. I think our team will enjoy the trip more now that we have this." Jaime held up his notebook and waved it in the air.

"Have fun, Jaime. I'll be at the site." He zipped up his bag and tapped his staff ID card on the scanner. The doors slid open and the two stepped out.

"Remember our flight leaves at eight, we could pick you up at the site and head to the airport together." Jaime waved him goodbye and Shohan continued on foot.

1500 B.C

Khai was about halfway back from Aswan. The smaller villages were starting to come into view from the days they had spent in the desert dunes. The ride back feels shorter. Maybe it was the fact that he would get to hold his Prince in his arms soon, he thought.

Zohar seemed to be in a light mood too. Khai would occasionally pat his warhorse's silky black mane and it would let out a cheery bray.

A sharp shrill scream rang in the skies and all heads

looked up to see a falcon circling above. It continued to let out its scream.

Horus.

Khai's heart stopped beating for a moment. The only time Horus would come flying to him was when the falcon failed to locate his Prince. He briefly saw a tied missive on the falcon's claws and he whistled into the sky.

Horus immediately flew towards him and perched itself onto Khai's shoulder. The latter frantically untied the missive.

Sevrin.

This is joyous news, my dear boy. We know the King of Egypt needed an heir and now he finally is expecting one.

I understand what you must be feeling. Warania is always your home, whenever you wish to return. You may stay for as long as you need until the King's heir is born.

Your father and I wish you a safe journey back home. I have missed you, my dear boy.

Mother.

Heir? What heir? Khai clenched the dried sheepskin in his hand. Something was not right. How was it possible for him to have an heir? He had never bedded his wife, unless...

Khai flared his nostrils and mounted Zohar. He may not be in love with the Begonian Princess, but she was still his wife. He would not sit still and watch his wife carry another man's child. And the fact that Horus could not find his Prince was a red flag.

"Rasiff!" Khai held on to Zohar's reins. Guards were immediately on high alert.

Rasiff, on his horse, strutted towards his King. "Yes, my King?"

"I want all guards to go back to the palace with me. NOW!" He commanded and watched his men ready their horses, swords, and spears.

It was not even sundown when Khai and their men started to see the palace coming into view. Zohar never once slowed down as they passed through Thebes, people clambered out of their way for Khai and his men. He even heard a couple of people scream and the sound of things knocking over.

Khai hurriedly dismounted Zohar before his warhorse

halted. Together with Rasiff and his throng of guards, Khai stomped into the empty throne room. It was eerily quiet, royal staff and even Plato were not here to receive his arrival.

He ran up the stairs to the West Wing. Horus immediately flew towards the study table and perched itself there like it always did.

The prince's chamber was empty. His Waranian Robe was laid over his chest of jewelleries. His bathing chamber did not have a single drop of water.

"My Prince!" Khai shouted, barging out of the bedchamber which he realized did not have his usual guards.

He was about to make his way to the East Wing when a man turned the corner and slammed into him, his tray of simples spilling onto the floor.

"I..I..forgive me, my King!"

Khai recognized the royal physician. Atum, who was his mother's personal physician and the one who delivered him when he was an infant.

"Where is everyone?!" Khai tried to not scream at the old man, his hands balled into fists.

Atum bowed and Khai saw the slight tremble in his frail old body. "Kafre, the Prince's guard, is in the infirmary! He is badly wounded!"

"Why was he? Where is the prince?!" He towered over the physician.

Atum hurriedly bent down to collect the spilled simples before straightening up with a slight bow to his King and spoke in a tremor, "You have to see Kafre, my King. Her Highness is with him! She is holding him captive!"

Khai could see Atum's reddened eyes as if he had been crying.

Without another word, Khai and his men made their way to the infirmary.

"My King!"

The Begonian Princess was the first to receive him in the infirmary. Khai saw guards around a bed and the person lying down on it with a scarred face.

Kafre.

"What happened to him! Where is Prince Sevrin!" Khai let his eyes roam around the infirmary, he would not forgive himself or anyone else if his Prince laid in one of these beds.

"He left—" The Princess spoke but was interrupted by another.

"Lies! Her men were hunting down the prince! Ugh!" Kafre tried to speak but a guard was pointing a dagger at his throat.

"What is the meaning of this!" Khai roared and watched his wife curl her lips into a smile.

"The Waranian Prince you loved so dearly, was carrying a child. He is a monster. He is an abomination, the Gods you are so devoted to, will not recognize him as a royal, it was his punishment for sleeping with your guard while you were away."

Kafre gritted his teeth, "It is not true! My King! I would never hurt the prince!" He yelled and eyed the guard's dagger. He had spent years in Assyria training to be a King's guard. Now that he knew his trusted men were here, he could finally attack, they now outnumbered the Princess' guards. Kafre, in one swift move, disarmed the guard before him. He grabbed the dagger and sliced through the guard's throat. "She sent men with bows and arrows after the Waranian Prince! It was murder!"

Khai reached out and grabbed the Princess' throat. "I knew it was you! You were the one who poisoned my mother's tea! You were killing her slowly! And now you took my Prince..." he kept walking forward until her back hit the wall of the infirmary and a soft clang on the granite floor was heard.

Khai looked down to see a piece of jewellery that had fallen out from the Princess' sash. It was a pure gold body chain which Khai recognized. He remembered seeing his Prince wearing this on several occasions. "Why do you have this!" He spoke through gritted teeth, fingers tightening his hold around the Princess' neck.

Nari shrugged and let out a burst of beseeching laughter. "For a King, you are slow-witted and weak. My Father did not marry me off to tighten our allies."

Khai tightened his grab and pushed his wife back until her head hit the wall. She winced but did not stop smiling.

"You should ready your men. The Begonian army is marching here as we speak. The Kingdom of Egypt shall be ours to reign!" She let out a menacing laughter Khai had never heard before.

Khai's eyes were bloodshot. "Where. Is. The. Prince." He spoke through gritted teeth, his nails digging into her neck. "WHERE DID YOU TAKE HIM!!!" His deep voice echoed around the infirmary.

Nari curled a side of her lips into a smirk. "He should have been swallowed up by the desert sand by now. A man with a swollen belly cannot run far, *my King*." She spat with sarcasm.

"Guards! Seize them!"

Spears and swords clanked. Kafre was limping but it did not take long for him and his men to put their spears and swords through the Princess' guards' chests.

Khai heard a tray fall on the granite floors and turn to see Atum by the infirmary's archway, blood draining from his face.

He strode towards the man. "Where is everyone else!"

Atum shakily replied, "In Jafaar's dungeon, my King! The Princess' guards had everyone tied up and held hostage!"

Khai, with one hand grabbing firmly onto the Princess' neck, held out one hand towards Kafre. The latter handed him his bloodied dagger.

"You will not do this!" The Begonian Princess spat, struggling to free herself from the Pharaoh's grasp. "The Gods will hear of this!" She screeched.

Khai had his jaw clenched tight, body heating up in rage as he gripped the handle of the dagger firmly, raising to the Princess' lips. "The Gods will not!" He slid the dagger past his wife's parted lips when she tried to retort.

The Princess' words came out in a series of indecipherable gargles with the dagger in her mouth.

Khai then forced the dagger down the back of her tongue, slicing the muscle off and the Princess cried in agony, mouth spilling with her own blood. "The Gods will not hear you speak, nor will they hear you beg for mercy and forgiveness!" Khai roared, withdrawing his dagger which was now pierced with the severed flesh of the Princess' tongue, and tossed it across the infirmary.

"Put her in a caged wagon! She shall be stripped of her royal title for committing high treason of the Queen Mother and the young Prince of Warania. She shall be publicly shamed and humiliated. She shall be stoned to death! And there shall be no public trial." Khai was panting with rage, his body was vibrating with the anger he was trying to contain.

He watched Kafre dragging the screaming Begonian Princess out of the infirmary. He had to find his Prince, wherever he may be.

The sun was starting to set low over the horizon. Khai was on his warhorse with Rasiff riding close by. He had searched everywhere, even the Valley of the Kings. His Prince was not in his burial chamber. Khai was too late, his heart clenched painfully in his chest as he reined Zohar to ride faster, far into the desert.

The sand dunes had changed with the high winds. All Khai saw was the vast piece of yellow sand. "My Prince..." Khai sobbed and screamed into the desert, his heart ached for his husband who was wrongfully murdered. The words of the Seer replayed in his head which only made more tears fall.

The day his feet touch the hot desert sand will be the day he takes his last breath.

Khai was not aware that the Seer was referring to his Prince. He cried and refused to stop. He reined Zohar and continued leading his horse further.

"My King!" Rasiff called after him. "You cannot do this, my King! The Begonian army is marching towards us, we have to prepare our men."

His guard was right. It was pointless to search for his Prince without any lead. Khai hated himself, he hated the position he was thrown in. As a King, he had to put aside his sorrows and continue to rule the Kingdom.

"I promise I will come back for you, my Prince. I promise I will search for you, no matter how long it takes me to…" Khai held onto his ruby necklace and whispered into the desert before reining Zohar to turn back to the palace.

After his royal staff, advisor, and court officials were released from the dungeon, he had everyone gathered in his study chamber. The atmosphere was quiet, everyone had learned about the Waranian Prince. Some, were even quietly shedding tears.

"I had sent missives to our allies. However, we need more men until they arrive. I need guards to come with me to the cities." Khai was motivated by rage, he had to protect his country.

"I will ready the men and horses," Rasiff said with a bow and left.

"I need food for five thousand men and maybe more," Khai instructed and the servants bowed and left for their duties.

"Ready our shields and weapons. We secure the perimeter before sundown." Khai watched Kafre delegating work to the other guards. With clenched fists and jaw, Khai looked out through his window shaft, gazed into the setting sun, and said, "it is war!"

Khai, together with his guards, rode their horses towards Thebes. The city had learned of the prince's murder. Commoners were on their knees as Khai and his men sat on their horses before them. He exchanged a look with Kafre and nodded.

Kafre reined his horse to step forward. "As all of you know, the Princess of Begonia had murdered the King's Prince."

Sniffles were heard.

"It was an attempt to overthrow the Great Pharaoh of Egypt. The accused will be held without a public trial and be stoned to death at first light."

Indecipherable angry yells went through the crowd.

"The army from the Kingdom of Begonia is marching towards us as we speak. There will be war on our land. We are here to seek more men before our allies could reach us." Kafre continued, watching the crestfallen eyes of the people. His heart clenched when he spotted the children the Waranian Prince frequently played with. "Men who can carry a hook, sword or spear, will fight alongside with our King to avenge the prince. Step forth if you wish to fight for your Prince, for your King, and for your country."

Khai watched his people cowered in fear. No one stepped forth but he spotted a slight movement within the crowd. People moved aside for a little boy. Khai recognized the boy, it was the same boy who presented a flower to his Prince during their wedding procession, the same boy who Khai saw playing with his Prince when he was dressed up as a palace guard.

Kafre swallowed thickly as a lump grew in his throat. The boy, named Ufu, with a wooden toy sword in hand, had stepped forth from the people, his eyes reddened and puffy. "I will fight for the prince," the boy spoke in his small voice.

Kafre dismounted from his horse and walked towards Ufu, kneeling to meet his height. "You are too young to fight, little one."

The boy, Ufu, scrunched up his face in agony before he wailed loudly, raising his hand to rub tears from his eyes as he cried. "They took away our Prince. I want to fight them! I want to! I am not a little boy!"

Khai could not help the tears that fell. Sniffles and cries could be heard growing louder after the spectacle from the little boy. Khai watched as grown men started standing up from the crowd and stepped forward. They must have been touched by the little boy's courage.

"I will fight!" A man in rags raised his clenched fist in the air.

Another man stepped forward. "I will fight too!"

More men volunteered to join the battle, some were noblemen, some were commoners, some were the homeless. "We will fight!"

Kafre's heart swelled. He knew the prince was well-loved by the people in Thebes, but he did not know the prince had such a big impact on them. Kafre mounted his horse and said, "All men willing to fight will be granted a position in the King's guard. Your families will be fed, your children will be clothed and given shelter."

Khai was touched by his people. He made a promise to himself that he would not surrender his land to the enemies, even though the Kingdom of Begonia had allies as big as his. He promised that he would protect his people. He would not fail this time.

CHAPTER 19

1500 B.C.

Khai, on his golden chariot pulled by his warhorse, stood on the frontlines. Gazing into the far distance of the desert from above the valleys, he could see the armies of Begonian soldiers marching through the desert, some were holding flags with the Begonian insignia. The Begonian general, whom Khai assumed to be the King of Begonia himself, rode centre on his own chariot pulled by his warhorse along the uneven desert sand dunes.

The valley gave Khai and his people leverage.

"Bows and arrows!" Khai yelled to his guards and soldiers.

The stretching of the ivory bows could be heard as his men readied their aim down to where his enemy and his troop of allies were.

Khai raised his hand in the air, jaw clenched tight, and commanded, "Release!"

Arrows hissed through the desert air and plunged down to the desert dunes. The Begonian army and their allies scattered, clearly disorganized and unprepared for the sudden attack.

"We advance!" Khai shouted and reined Zohar to pull his golden chariot with his troop of men behind him, armed with hooks, daggers, swords, spears, and shields.

While Khai and his men advanced down the valley, arrows were shot towards them, some men fell, some protected themselves with their shields. The Begonian troops were being centered— far in the desert horizons, Khai spotted a larger troop bigger than the Begonian armies and their allies approaching the desert land with their multiple coloured flags painted with their Kingdoms' insignia. His heart clenched painfully when he made out the black flag with golden insignia of Waranian armies leading their allies. He also spotted the blue insignia flag of the Kingdom of Saracca. Khai could count at least more than ten Kingdoms marching towards the Begonian troops.

"Shield wall!" Khai shouted when they reached the bottom of the valley. His men readied their shields with one hand, creating a line of border, while their other hand held onto their spears and swords.

Khai rode in the frontlines with Kafre and Rasiff. "Today, I stand before you, not as your King!" He reined Zohar along the shield wall his men created. "But as your General. Today!" He looked into the determined eyes of his men behind their shields, some already had blood caking a side of their face. "We avenge the prince!"

The men hooted in unison, banging their shields. "For the prince!" They yelled.

Khai could see the small shallow stream of river starting to fill the Nile, separating the Begonian troops and him with his allies across the river. It would not deter his allies, for he knew they were strong warriors.

Kafre rode beside him as their men readied themselves for the attack.

"Kafre, you do not have to protect—"

Kafre shook his head. "My King!"

Khai reached forward to grab his most loyal guard by his shoulder, giving it a firm squeeze. "As I have said, today I stand before you, not as your King. You will put your life before mine."

Kafre wanted to protest but his King strode forth in his chariot and unsheathed his sword from its scabbard by his waist, his veined arm clenched tight by its handle, every muscle in his body vibrating with rage.

"There shall be no mercy! Attack!" Khai screamed at his troops.

He took centre, he was unmerciful, every strike of his sword through his enemies' chests reminded him of his Prince. He only blamed himself for not being able to protect him. Khai rode on his rage and fought, fought, fought...

Present Day

His heart felt heavy as he climbed down the ladder to the tomb. Every step he took made him feel like he was leaving a part of him here.

Shohan did not understand the pull he had towards the entity. He could have informed his team the very first time he found the solid golden coffin, if he had, this tomb would have been emptied out by now, but he did not. In fact, the young archaeologist had found himself coming back here in search of the late Pharaoh. He should have feared him, but he was not. He should have been cursed when the entity screamed and disappeared on him, but he was not.

Standing before the archway, he took a deep shaky breath and entered.

It was pitch black and the air around smelled of stale

moss. "Khai…" he whispered, listening to his own echo.

He wondered if giving the Pharaoh the body chain had given him closure. If it did, he wondered if the entity would appear once more. He still had questions unanswered.

"I… came here to … say goodbye," Shohan felt his chest tightened as a lump grew in his throat. He took a deep breath, willing away the tears that were threatening to spill. "I am going home."

Nothing. The burial chamber was quiet.

He sighed and turned around. Maybe the late Pharaoh had returned to his netherworld to rule Egypt as the myths said.

Shohan had a foot out of the archway when he saw brightness before seeing his own shadow casting before him. With a gasp, he turned frantically to see the fire torches lit, the Pharaoh, warm bronze chest glistening under the firelight, his ruby necklace sparkling, stood before him, and his kohl-lined eyes bored into his.

"Khai…" Shohan sobbed, taking slow steps towards the Pharaoh, whose eyes never left his as he approached the latter.

The archaeologist knew he was not the Prince the Pharaoh sought, but he would not deny that during this period where he had come down to Khai Tutankhamen's tomb in search of him, he had grown slightly attached to the entity.

"My… Prince…" the Pharaoh's voice was still filled with agony, though his eyes seemed hopeful to see him. "I have missed you," the Pharaoh opened his arms wide for him and Shohan ran towards the entity and let him curl his veiny arms around his waist.

He let himself be held tight by the Pharaoh, face squished against his chest. He heard the Pharaoh taking a deep breath, chest rising and falling. It felt odd to have his face buried in one's chest without hearing his heartbeat. Part of him wanted to know how the Pharaoh's heartbeat sounded, though he knew it was not possible, for the Pharaoh was not alive.

Shohan peeled himself away and as if he was guided by a spirit, he found himself tipping his toes to reach the Pharaoh's height and captured the entity's lips with his. He felt the Pharaoh's long exhale on his philtrum when the latter deepened their kiss.

When they broke apart, his heart was hammering wildly in his chest. Shohan did not know what came over him that made him behave that way.

"Khai, I came to say goodbye," Shohan said timidly, the Pharaoh's arms immediately curled around him protectively.

Pharaoh Khai's expression was sullen upon hearing him say that. "Do you really have to go?"

Shohan winced, he had missed the Pharaoh's deep authoritative voice. He remembered the Pharaoh making him feel safe in his arms when he was still traumatized by the tomb raiders.

He nodded, placing a hand on the Pharaoh's cheek and watched the firelight dance in the reflection of his warm brown orbs. "I know you took tomb raiders. You did, right?"

The mention of the tomb raiders made a shift in the Pharaoh's eyes, he briefly saw the entity's expression hardened. "They tried to hurt you. I promised whoever had the intention of causing you harm, shall meet my wrath."

Shohan felt the dots connecting in his head. The myths were true, that the ancient Egyptian Pharaohs now ruled the land in their afterlife.

He swallowed the lump in his throat. "The prince, the body chain..." he trailed off studying the Pharaoh's expression. "I hope you find him, wherever he may be."

The Pharaoh closed his eyes and Shohan thought he saw wetness in the entity's lashes. It knifed his heart.

"I was not able to find... him," the Pharaoh said and Shohan felt the hold on him tightened. "But I managed to find you," the Pharaoh reached up and caressed his cheek before swiping away a lock of hair that was falling over his eyes. The archaeologist's heart fluttered.

Shohan let his palm press against the hand that was caressing his cheek. "Khai... you do know I am not the prince you seek, right?"

He briefly saw the Pharaoh clench his jaw tight before giving him a nod.

"Then tell me, Khai... how did you... die?" He asked the question that had been bugging him for years.

The Pharaoh let out a shaky exhale, his kohl-lined eyes unwilling to meet him as he spoke, "I am not proud... of how I passed."

Shohan did not know what the Pharaoh meant. If he was not proud of how he had died, it only meant he did not die on the battlefield.

"Then was it true? That the... child, the prince was carrying... was... yours?"

The Pharaoh took a deep breath as he took the archaeologist's hand and forced his fingers open before placing it on his sternum. Shohan felt as if this was what the late Prince often did, he wondered if the Pharaoh found this affection as a way of calming himself down. "I was told so, but I did not believe it then. But when you brought it up, I knew it had to be true, that the prince, that my beautiful, beautiful beloved Prince, was carrying my child, our child..."

Shohan gasped. "So, the Great Pharaoh of Egypt, the last King who ruled the Middle Empire, had an heir."

The ground shook and dust fell on their heads. Shohan whimpered as the Pharaoh held him tight.

It was an earthquake. He could hear the faint sound of rubble and stones crashing and echoing around the burial chamber. "We have to leave," Shohan subconsciously grabbed Pharaoh Khai's arms and dragged him but his weight was too strong. He turned back to the Pharaoh, worried.

He watched the Pharaoh unclasped his ruby necklace,

holding it in his calloused palms.

"This was said to have been blessed by the high priest of Valharia, it was said to protect its wearer from all evils." The Pharaoh clasped the necklace around the young archaeologist's neck.

Shohan had his heart in his mouth. More dust fell on their heads and part of a stonewall in the burial chamber crashed on the ground behind them. He whimpered as the Pharaoh grabbed his chin and pulled him in for a deep kiss. Shohan let his fingers card through the Pharaoh's coarse hair, pulling his nape closer as they shared their last kiss. "Khai..." he began to cry when the Pharaoh pulled away and pried his hands away from him.

Pharaoh Khai's eyes were teary as he let his hand caress the softness of his cheek. "I failed to protect him the last time. I will not have the same thing happen to you. Go!"

Shohan took a step forward but the Pharaoh only pushed him towards the archway. "Go, my Prince. Be safe..."

More stone walls fell and Shohan tipped his toes and placed a chaste kiss on the Pharaoh's lips for the final time.

He reluctantly turned and ran out of the chamber. Some limestone walls in the narrow tunnel shafts had blocked his way. Tears rolled down his cheek as he replayed his last moments with the entity while he pried away the stone walls. Shohan lifted his collar and tugged the ruby between his chest and shirt. He did not want to lose it.

"He is here! He is here!"

Shohan gasped at the familiar voice.

"Jaime? Help!" Shohan cried as he tried prodding at the fallen stones.

"Heave!"

He heard several familiar voices shouted. Shocks after shocks rocked the round and Shohan found himself trapped in the tunnel shaft. He was so close to the opening.

Light spilled into the tunnel when a huge stone wall was removed from the opposite direction. He felt a hand reached towards where he was and grabbed his arm.

He was pulled out of the tunnel but his mind was dazed. He needed oxygen, he needed water.

"He is alright! Slight scratches, but he is alright!"

Shohan gasped for air as his colleagues placed him on the desert sand. They offered him water and he took a huge gulp.

"Are you okay? You got everyone so worried!" Jaime spoke and swept off the dust on his head.

He nodded.

"Luckily we were already near the excavation site when the first tremor shook. Jaime said you went back down to the tomb again, we ran here as fast as we could." Layton panted, back hunched and palms resting on his knees.

"I am... I am okay." He reassured them, though his voice was shaking.

"You sure?" Jaime added, he still seemed worried and continued to roam his eyes on his arms to check for any visible injuries.

He nodded. When he turned back to the opening of the tomb, he saw that it was covered by desert sand and boulders of stones. He wondered what happened to the Pharaoh, the entity. His chest tightened thinking of the Pharaoh's final words to him.

As he and his team began to walk back to Layton's rented car, Shohan turned towards where Khai Tutankhamen's tomb was. He watched the sun that was starting to set beyond the valley's horizon and gasped. He saw the silhouette of a man wearing a headpiece with a feline by its heel high up in the valley. Shohan reached up and pressed his palm against where the ruby rested against his chest as he let one last tear fall, watching the silhouette of Pharaoh Khai and the feline.

"Goodbye, Khai..." he whispered as the wind began to pick up and swirls of sand began clouding around the silhouettes. "I'll see you again... farewell... *my King*..."

Shohan watched the swirls of sand get picked up by the high winds and the silhouettes gradually faded into the growing sandstorm.

He turned his back on the valley with a heavy heart as he followed his team. A shrill scream came from above and Shohan looked up to see a bird circling above them, it looked like an eagle, or maybe a falcon, the archaeologist could not be sure. As he walked and walked, tears began falling again.

When his team asked again if he was okay, Shohan only lied and said that he was just traumatized from the earlier earthquake rescue.

"You are okay. We are here. It is going to be alright."

He let Jaime's words calm him as they approached their vehicle that would take them to the airport.

1500 B.C

Khai huffed, mildly wounded, as he held onto his bloodied sword, looking out to the sea of fallen soldiers lying lifeless on the desert sand. They had defeated Begonia and their allies, though some of his men did not survive. Khai had given out orders for his guards to pull up their own men who had died on the battlefield to be honourably mummified and to be placed to rest in the burial chamber underneath his own.

He mounted Zohar as he watched bodies floating on the Nile which was now red with both his men and his enemies' blood.

The Nile will flood once more. However, it will be filled with the blood of your people and your foes.

The Seer's words repeatedly rang in his head. His chest tightened. If only Khai had immediately turned and rode back to the palace after encountering the Seer, he could have saved his Prince. But it was all too late now, Khai could only blame himself.

Khai saw the shadow of a bird circling on the desert sand and looked up to see Horus. He put two fingers in his mouth and whistled.

When Horus perched himself on his veined and wounded arm, Khai stroked the falcon's feather and looked into its heterochromia eyes. "Fly freely, Horus. Go, watch over the prince, wherever he may be…" Khai swung his arm upwards and watched Horus soared into the sky, far into the horizon of the setting sun.

1499 B.C

Khai spent the next year restoring his country after his Prince's death and winning the war. His country prospered, the Nile flooded once again and traders across seas docked their boats along the riverbank.

He dismissed Plato and his court officials after he was done with his duties.

Khai took the stairs up to the North Wing. He had not been there since his mother's death. He took a look around her bed chamber and spotted something glimmering between the slit of her closet doors. He opened it and saw a small golden throne where he once sat when he was a child. He never knew his mother still kept it.

With one final look around his mother's bedchamber, Khai left, taking a turn towards the West Wing.

On his way, he saw his guard, Kafre, having light conversations with a much older chambermaid. It was Kafre's mother.

"You are smiling, Rasiff. You never smiled."

He heard a man's voice and turned to see a guard resting his arm over Rasiff's shoulders. The latter then smirked and replied, "Humped my woman all night."

Khai sighed heavily as he reached the prince's bedchambers. He reminisced the days where his Prince would beam brightly and run up to him when the day's duties were done. Now, he had no family to return to.

After his Prince's death, Khai never returned to his own bedchamber. It reminded him too much of their time together and it tore him to pieces. He looked out through the window shaft, the sun was setting, the lights from Thebes slowly diminishing as his people headed home to their families.

You are now my family too, my Prince.

Khai remembered the words he said to his husband not long after their wedding. He missed his Prince so dearly that Khai hardly smiled or ate anymore.

He sighed and walked over to a shelf where he recently acquired a vial of potion from a street sorcerer when he visited Thebes, secretly dressed as a commoner.

He laid on the soft bed where his Prince once slept and let a single tear fall. "I promise I will search for you, my Prince," Khai whispered to himself in the lonely cold chamber as he untwisted the vial's cork and watched the blackened liquid swirl within the glass.

"If I cannot find you in this realm, I will search for you in the other," Khai smiled faintly, hopeful to see his Prince once again as he placed the opening of the vial on his lips and chugged down its contents.

"It is a promise to you, my beautiful, beautiful Prince..."

The End.
To be continued....

Printed in Great Britain
by Amazon